VAMPIRE MOUNTAIN

THE SAGA OF DARREN SHAN
BOOK 4

Other titles by
DARREN SHAN

THE SAGA OF DARREN SHAN

1 Cirque Du Freak*
2 The Vampire's Assistant*
3 Tunnels of Blood*
4 Vampire Mountain
5 Trials of Death
6 The Vampire Prince
7 Hunters of the Dusk
8 Allies of the Night
9 Killers of the Dawn
10 The Lake of Souls
11 Lord of the Shadows
12 Sons of Destiny

THE DEMONATA

1 Lord Loss*
2 Demon Thief*
3 Slawter*
4 Bec*
5 Blood Beast*
6 Demon Apocalypse*
7 Death's Shadow*
8 Wolf Island*

Also available on audio

DARREN SHAN
VAMPIRE MOUNTAIN

THE SAGA OF DARREN SHAN
BOOK 4

HarperCollins *Children's Books*

If your trip to Vampire Mountain leaves you bloodthirsty for more, visit www.darrenshan.com

First published in Great Britain by HarperCollins *Children's Books* 2001
This edition published 2009
HarperCollins *Children's Books* is a division of HarperCollins*Publishers* Ltd,
77-85 Fulham Palace Road, Hammersmith,
London W6 8JB

The HarperCollins website address is:
www.harpercollins.co.uk

5

Text copyright © 2001 Darren Shan

ISBN-13   978 0 00 793896 4

The author asserts the moral right to
be identified as the author of the work.

Printed and bound in England by
CPI Group (UK) Ltd, Croydon CR0 4YY

For:

The Freaky Fitzes: Ronan, Lorcan, Kealan, Tiernan & Meara
— viva the Shack Pack!!!

OBEs (Order of the Bloody Entrails) to:
Ann "the monstervator" Murphy
Moira "the mediatrix" Reilly
Tony "giggsy" Purdue

Partners In Crime:
Liam & Biddy
Gillie & Zoë
Emma & Chris

PROLOGUE

"PACK YOUR bags," Mr Crepsley said late one night, as he was heading for his coffin. "We leave for Vampire Mountain tomorrow."

I was used to the vampire making declarations out of the blue – he didn't believe in consulting me when making up his mind – but this was extraordinary, even for him.

"*Vampire Mountain?*" I shrieked, racing after him. "Why are we going *there?*"

"To present you to the Council," he said. "It is time."

"The Council of Vampire Generals?" I asked. "Why do we have to go? Why now?"

"We go because it is proper," he said. "And we go now because the Council only meets once every twelve years. If we miss this year's gathering, we will have a long wait until the next."

And that was all he'd say about it. He turned a deaf ear to

the rest of my questions and tucked himself into his coffin before the sun rose, leaving me to fret the day away.

* * *

My name's Darren Shan. I'm a half-vampire. I used to be human until eight or so years ago, when my destiny clashed with Mr Crepsley's and I reluctantly became his assistant. I had a hard time adapting to the vampire and his ways — especially when it came to drinking human blood — but finally I resigned myself, accepted my lot, and got on with the business of living.

We were part of a travelling band of amazing circus performers, led by a man called Hibernius Tall. We toured the world, putting on incredible shows for customers who appreciated our strange and magical talents.

Six years had passed since Mr Crepsley and me had last been separated from the Cirque Du Freak. We'd left to put a stop to a mad vampaneze by the name of Murlough, who was terrorizing the vampire's home city. The vampaneze are a breakaway group of vampires who kill humans when they feed on them. Vampires don't — we just take a bit of blood and move on, leaving those we sup from unharmed. Most of the vampire myths you read about in books or see in films actually originated with the vampaneze.

They'd been a good six years. I'd become a regular performer at the Cirque, going on with Madam Octa — Mr Crepsley's poisonous spider — every night to amaze and frighten audiences. I'd also learnt a few magic tricks, which I'd worked into the act. I got on well with the rest of the Cirque troupe. I'd grown accustomed to the wandering lifestyle and had been enjoying myself.

Now, after six years of stability, we were about to journey into the unknown again. I knew a small bit about the Council and Vampire Mountain. Vampires were ruled by soldiers called Vampire Generals who made sure their laws were enforced. They killed mad or evil vampires and kept the rest of the walking un-dead in line. Mr Crepsley used to be a Vampire General, but quit long ago, for reasons he'd never revealed.

Every so often — I now knew it was twelve years — the Generals gathered at a secret fortress to discuss whatever it was that blood-sucking creatures of the night discussed when they got together. Not only Generals attended — I'd heard that ordinary vampires could go as well — but they made up the majority. I didn't know where the fortress was, or how we'd get there, or why I had to be presented to the Council — but I was about to find out!

CHAPTER ONE

I WAS excited but anxious about the journey – I was venturing into the unknown, and I'd a feeling it wouldn't prove to be a smooth trip – so I spent the day busily packing rucksacks for myself and Mr Crepsley, to make the time pass faster. (Full-vampires will die if exposed to the sun for more than a few hours, but half-vampires aren't affected by it.) Since I didn't know where we were going, I didn't know what to take or leave. If Vampire Mountain was icy and wintry, I'd need thick clothes and boots; if it was somewhere hot and tropical, T-shirts and shorts would be more in order.

I asked some of the Cirque people about it but they knew nothing, except Mr Tall, who said I should pack for snow. Mr Tall was one of those people who seem to know something about everything.

Evra agreed about the snow. "I doubt if sun-shy vampires would make their base in the Caribbean!" he snorted.

Evra Von was a snake-boy, with scales instead of skin. Rather, he *used* to be a snake-boy — now he was a snake-*man*. Evra had grown these last six years, got taller and broader and older-looking. I hadn't. As a half-vampire, I aged at one-fifth the normal rate. So, though eight years had passed since Mr Crepsley blooded me, I only looked a year or so older.

I hated not being able to grow normally. Evra and me used to be best buddies, but not any more. We were still good friends and shared a tent, but he was a young man now, more interested in people — particularly women! — his own age. In reality I was only a couple of years younger than Evra, but I looked like a kid, and it was difficult for him to treat me as an equal.

There were benefits to being a half-vampire — I was stronger and faster than any human, and would live longer — but I'd have given them all up if it meant looking my real age and being able to lead an ordinary life.

Even though Evra and me were no longer as close as we'd once been, he was still my friend, and was worried about me heading off for Vampire Mountain. "From what I know, that journey's no joke," he warned in the deep voice which hit him a few years ago. "Maybe I should come with you."

I'd have loved to jump at his offer, but Evra had his own life to lead. It wouldn't be fair to drag him away from the Cirque Du Freak. "No," I told him. "Stay and keep my hammock warm. I'll be OK. Besides, snakes don't like the cold, do they?"

"That's true," he laughed. "I'd most likely fall asleep and hibernate till spring!"

Even though Evra wouldn't be coming, he helped me pack. I didn't have much to take: spare clothes, a thick pair of boots, special cooking utensils which folded up neatly so they were easier to carry, my diary – that went everywhere with me – and other bits and pieces. Evra told me to take a rope — he said it might come in handy, especially when it came to climbing.

"But vampires are great climbers," I reminded him.

"I know," he said, "but do you really want to hang off the side of a mountain with only your fingertips for support?"

"Of course he does!" someone boomed behind us before I could answer. "Vampires thrive on danger."

Turning to see who it was, I found myself face to face with the sinister being known as Mr Tiny, and my insides instantly froze with fright.

Mr Tiny was a small, plump man, with white hair, thick glasses and a pair of green wellies. He often toyed with a heart-shaped watch. He looked like a kindly old uncle but was in fact a cruel, dark-hearted man, who'd cut your tongue out as soon as say "hello". Nobody knew much about him, but everyone was afraid of him. His first name was Desmond, and if you shortened it and put it together with his surname you got *Mr Destiny*.

I hadn't seen Mr Tiny since shortly after joining the Cirque Du Freak, but I'd heard many tales about him – how he ate children for breakfast, and burned down towns to warm his feet. My heart tightened when I saw him standing a few metres away, eyes twinkling, hands wrapped behind his back, eavesdropping on Evra and me.

"Vampires are peculiar creatures," he said, stepping forward, as though he'd been part of the conversation all along. "They love a challenge. I knew one once who walked himself to death in sunlight, merely because someone had sneered at him for only being able to come out at night."

He stuck out a hand and, scared as I was, I automatically shook it. Evra didn't — when Mr Tiny extended his hand to the snake-man, he stood, quivering, shaking his head furiously. Mr Tiny merely smiled and withdrew the hand.

"So, you're off to Vampire Mountain," he said, picking up my rucksack and peering inside without asking. "Take matches, Master Shan. The way is long and the days are cold. The winds that gust around Vampire Mountain would cut even a tough-skinned young man like you to the bone."

"Thanks for the advice," I said.

That was the confusing thing about Mr Tiny: he was always polite and amiable, so even if you knew he was the sort of man who wouldn't blink in the face of great evil, you couldn't help liking him at least some of the time.

"Are my Little People near?" he asked. The Little People were short creatures who dressed in blue robes with hoods, never spoke, and ate anything that moved (including humans!). A handful of the mysterious beings almost always travelled with the Cirque Du Freak, and there were eight of them with us at that time.

"They're probably in their tent," I said. "I took them in some food an hour or so ago and I think they're still eating." One of my jobs was to hunt for the Little People. Evra used to do it with me, until he grew up and demanded less messy chores. Nowadays I was helped by a couple of young humans, children of the Cirque helpers.

"Excellent," Mr Tiny beamed, and started away. "Oh," he paused, "one last thing. Tell Larten not to leave until I've had a word with him."

"I think we're in a hurry," I said. "We might not have time to—"

"Just tell him I want a word," Mr Tiny interrupted. "I'm sure he'll make time for *me*." With that, he tipped his glasses at us, waved farewell and moved on. I shared a worried look with Evra, found some matches and stuck them in my bag, then hurried off to wake Mr Crepsley.

CHAPTER TWO

MR CREPSLEY was snappish when I woke him — he hated rising before the sun went down — but stopped complaining when I explained why I'd disturbed his sleep. "Mr Tiny," he sighed, scratching the long scar which ran down the left side of his face. "I wonder what *he* wants?"

"I don't know," I answered, "but he said not to leave until he'd had a word with you." I lowered my voice and whispered, "We could sneak away without being seen if we hurried. Twilight's not far off. You could stand an hour or so of sunlight if we kept to the shadows, couldn't you?"

"I could," Mr Crepsley agreed, "were I given to fleeing like a dog with its tail between its legs. But I am not. I will face Desmond Tiny. Bring me my finest cloak — I like to look my best for visitors." That was as close to a joke as the vampire was likely to come — he didn't have much of a sense of humour.

An hour later, with the sun setting, we made our way to Mr Tall's caravan, where Mr Tiny was regaling the owner of the Cirque Du Freak with tales of what he'd seen in a recent earthquake.

"Ah, Larten!" Mr Tiny boomed. "Prompt as ever."

"Desmond," Mr Crepsley replied stiffly.

"Have a seat," Mr Tiny said.

"Thank you, but I will stand." Nobody liked sitting when Mr Tiny was around — in case they needed to make a quick getaway.

"I hear you're casting off for Vampire Mountain," Mr Tiny said.

"We leave presently," Mr Crepsley confirmed.

"This is the first Council you've been to in nearly fifty years, isn't it?"

"You are well informed," Mr Crepsley grunted.

"I keep an ear to the ground."

There was a knock at the door, and Mr Tall admitted two of the Little People. One walked with a slight limp. He'd been with the Cirque Du Freak almost as long as me. I called him Lefty, though that was only a nickname — none of the Little People had real names.

"Ready, boys?" Mr Tiny asked. The Little People nodded. "Excellent!" He smiled at Mr Crepsley. "The path to Vampire Mountain is as hazardous as ever, isn't it?"

"It is not easy," Mr Crepsley agreed cagily.

"Dangerous for a young snip of a thing like Master Shan, wouldn't you say?"

"Darren can look after himself," Mr Crepsley said, and I grinned proudly.

"I'm sure he can," Mr Tiny responded, "but it's unusual for one so young to make the journey, isn't it?"

"Yes," Mr Crepsley said curtly.

"That's why I'm sending these two along as guards." Mr Tiny waved a hand at the Little People.

"*Guards?*" Mr Crepsley barked. "We do not need any. I have made the trip many times. I can look after Darren myself."

"You can indeed," Mr Tiny cooed, "but a little help never went astray, did it?"

"They would get in the way," Mr Crepsley growled. "I do not want them."

"My Little People? Get in the way?" Mr Tiny sounded shocked. "They exist only to serve. They'll be like shepherds, watching over the two of you while you sleep."

"Nevertheless," Mr Crepsley insisted, "I do not want—"

"This is not an offer," Mr Tiny interrupted. Though he spoke softly, the menace in his voice was unmistakable. "They're going with you. End of story. They'll hunt for themselves and see to their own sleeping arrangements. All you have to do is make sure you don't 'lose' them in the snowy wastelands on the way."

"And when we get there?" Mr Crepsley snapped. "Do you expect me to take them inside? That is not permitted. The Princes will not stand for it."

"Yes they will," Mr Tiny disagreed. "Don't forget by

whose hands the Hall of Princes was built. Paris Skyle and the rest know on which side their blood is buttered. They won't object."

Mr Crepsley was furious – practically shaking with rage – but the anger seeped out of him as he stared into Mr Tiny's eyes and realized there was no arguing with the little man. In the end he nodded and averted his gaze, ashamed at having to bow to the demands of this interfering man.

"I knew you'd see it my way," Mr Tiny beamed, then turned his attention to me. "You've grown," he noted. "Inside, where it matters. Your battles with the Wolf Man and Murlough have toughened you."

"How do you know about that?" Mr Crepsley gasped. It was common knowledge that I'd had a run-in with the fearsome Wolf Man, but nobody was meant to know of our fight with Murlough. If the vampaneze ever found out, they'd hunt us to the ends of the Earth and kill us.

"I know all manner of things," Mr Tiny cackled. "This world holds no secrets from me. You've come a long way," he addressed me again, "but there's a long way yet to go. The path ahead isn't easy, and I'm not just talking about the route to Vampire Mountain. You must be strong, and keep faith in yourself. Never admit defeat, even when it seems inevitable."

I hadn't expected such a speech, and I listened in a daze, numbly wondering why he was sharing such words with me.

"That's all I have to say," he finished, standing and rubbing his heart-shaped watch. "Time's ticking. We've all got places to be and deadlines to meet. I'll be on my way.

Hibernius, Larten, Darren." He bowed briefly to each of us in turn. "We'll meet again, I'm sure." He turned, headed for the door, shared a look with the Little People, then let himself out. In the silence which followed, we stared at one another speechlessly, wondering what all that had been about.

* * *

Mr Crepsley wasn't happy but he couldn't postpone leaving — making it to the Council on time was more important than anything else, he told me. So, while the Little People stood waiting outside his van, I helped him pack.

"Those clothes will not do," he said, referring to my bright pirate costume which still fitted me after all the years of wear and tear. "Where we are going, you would stand out like a peacock. Here," he thrust a bundle at me. I unrolled it to reveal a light grey jumper and trousers, along with a woolly cap.

"How long have you been preparing for this?" I asked.

"Some time now," he admitted, pulling on clothes of a similar colour to mine, in place of his usual red attire.

"Couldn't you have told me about it earlier?"

"I could have," he replied in that infuriating way of his.

I slipped into my new clothes, then looked for socks and shoes. Mr Crepsley shook his head when he saw me searching. "No footwear," he said. "We go barefoot."

"Over snow and ice?" I yelped.

"Vampires have harder feet than humans," he said. "You will barely feel the cold, especially when we are walking."

"What about stones and thorns?" I grumbled.

"They will toughen your soles up even more," he grinned, then took off his slippers. "It is the same for all vampires. The way to Vampire Mountain is not just a journey — it is a test. Boots, jackets, ropes: such items are not permitted."

"Sounds crazy to me," I sighed, but took the rope, spare clothes and boots out of my bag. When we were ready, Mr Crepsley asked where Madam Octa was. "You're not bringing *her*, are you?" I grumbled — I knew who'd have to look after her if she came, and it wouldn't be Mr Crepsley!

"There is someone I wish to show her to," he said.

"Someone who eats spiders, I hope," I sniffed, but fetched her from behind his coffin, where I kept her between shows. She shuffled around while I lifted the cage and placed it in my bag, but settled down once she found herself in the dark again.

Then it was time to go. I'd said goodbye to Evra earlier — he was taking part in that night's show and had to prepare — and Mr Crepsley had bid farewell to Mr Tall. Nobody else would miss us.

"Ready?" Mr Crepsley asked.

"Ready," I sighed.

Leaving the safety of the van, we cleared the camp, let the two silent Little People fall into place behind us, and set off on what would prove to be a wild, peril-filled adventure into lands cold and foreign and steeped in blood.

CHAPTER THREE

I WOKE shortly before nightfall, stretched the stiffness out of my bones — what I wouldn't have given for a bed or hammock! — then left the confines of the cave to study the barren land we were journeying through. I didn't get much chance to study the countryside while we travelled at night. It was only during quiet moments such as these that I could pause and take everything in.

We hadn't hit the snowlands yet, but already we'd left most of civilization behind. Humans were few and far between out here where the ground was rocky and forbidding. Even animals were scarce, though some were strong enough to eke out a living — mostly deer, wolves and bears.

We'd been travelling for weeks, maybe a month — I lost track of time after the first handful of nights. Whenever I asked Mr Crepsley how many kilometres were left, he'd smile and say, "We are some way off yet."

My feet cut up badly when we reached the hard ground. Mr Crepsley applied the sap of herbal plants that he found along the way to my soles, carried me for a few nights while my skin grew back (I healed quicker than a human would), and I'd been OK since.

I said one night that it was a pity the Little People were with us, or he could have carried me on his back and flitted. (Vampires are able to run at an extra-fast speed, a magic kind of running, where they slip through space like eels through a net. They call it 'flitting'.) He said our slow pace had nothing to do with the Little People. "Flitting is not permitted on the way to Vampire Mountain," he explained. "The journey is a way of weeding out the weak from the strong. Vampires are ruthless in certain aspects. We do not believe in supporting those who are incapable of supporting themselves."

"That's not very nice," I observed. "What about somebody who's old or injured?"

Mr Crepsley shrugged. "Either they do not attempt the journey, or they die trying."

"That's stupid," I said. "If I could flit, I would. No one would know."

The vampire sighed. "You still do not understand our ways," he said. "There is no nobility in pulling the wool over the eyes of one's comrades. We are proud beings, Darren, who live by exacting codes. From our point of view it is better to lose one's life than lose one's pride."

Mr Crepsley often spoke about pride and nobility and being true to oneself. Vampires were a stern lot, he said, who lived as close to nature as they could. Their lives were rarely easy, and that was the way they liked it — "Life is a challenge," he once told me, "and only those who rise to the challenge truly know what it means to live."

I'd grown accustomed to the Little People, who trailed along behind us at night, silent, aloof, precise. They hunted for their own food during the day, while we slept. By the time we woke, they'd eaten and grabbed a few hours sleep and were ready to go. Their pace never changed. They marched behind us like robots, a few metres to the rear. I thought the one with the limp might struggle, but he'd yet to show signs that he was feeling any strain.

Mr Crepsley and me fed mostly on deer. Their blood was hot, salty and good. We had bottles of human blood to keep us going — vampires need regular doses of human blood to remain healthy, and though they prefer to drink directly from the vein, they can bottle blood and store it — but we drank from them sparingly, saving them in case of an emergency.

Mr Crepsley wouldn't let me light a fire in the open — it might attract attention — but it was allowed in way-stations. Way-stations were caves or underground caverns where bottles of human blood and coffins were stored. They were resting places, where vampires could hole up for a day or two. There weren't many of them — it took about a week to make it from one to another — and some had been taken over or destroyed by animals since Mr Crepsley had last come this way.

"How come they allow way-stations but no shoes or

ropes?" I asked one day as we warmed our feet by a fire and tucked into roast venison (we ate it raw most of the time).

"The way-stations were introduced after our war with the vampaneze seven hundred years ago," he said. "We lost many of our clan in the fight with the vampaneze, and humans killed even more of us. Our numbers were dangerously low. The way-stations were set up to make it easier to get to Vampire Mountain. Some vampires object to them and never use them, but most accept them."

"How many vampires *are* there?" I asked.

"Between two and three thousand," he answered. "Maybe a few hundred more or less."

I whistled. "That's a lot!"

"Three thousand is nothing," he snorted. "Think about the billions of humans."

"It's more than I expected," I said.

"Once, we numbered more than a hundred thousand," Mr Crepsley said. "And this was long ago, when that was a huge amount."

"What happened to them?" I asked.

"They were killed," he sighed. "Humans with stakes; disease; fights — vampires love to fight. In the centuries before the vampaneze broke away and provided us with a real foe, we fought amongst ourselves, many dying in duels. We came close to extinction, but kept our heads above water, just about."

"How many Vampire Generals are there?" I asked curiously.

"Between three and four hundred."

"And vampaneze?"

"Maybe two hundred and fifty, or three hundred — I cannot say for sure."

As I was remembering this old conversation, Mr Crepsley emerged from the cave behind me and watched the sun sinking. It looked the same colour as his cropped orange hair. The vampire was in great form — the nights were growing longer the closer to Vampire Mountain we got, so he was able to move about more than usual.

"It is always nice to see it go down," Mr Crepsley said, referring to the sun.

"I thought it was going to snow earlier," I said.

"There will be snow aplenty soon," he replied. "We should reach the snow drifts this week." He glanced down at my feet. "Will you be able to survive the harsh cold?"

"I've made it this far, haven't I?"

"This has been the easy part," he smiled, then clapped me on the back when he saw my dismayed frown. "Do not worry — you will be fine. But let me know if your feet cut up again. There are rare bushes which grow along the trail, the sap of which can seal the pores of one's skin."

The Little People came out of the cave, hoods covering their faces. The one without a limp was carrying a dead fox.

"Ready?" Mr Crepsley asked me.

I nodded and swung my rucksack on to my back. Looking ahead over the rocky terrain, I asked the usual question: "Is it much further?"

Mr Crepsley smiled, began walking, and said over his shoulder, "We are some way off yet."

Muttering darkly, I glanced back at the relatively comfortable cave, then faced front and followed the vampire. The Little People fell in behind, and after a while I heard brittle snapping sounds as they chewed on the bones of the fox.

* * *

Four nights later we ran into heavy snow. For a few nights we travelled over country that was one long unbroken blanket of freezing white, where nothing lived, but after that trees, plants and animals appeared again.

My feet felt like two blocks of ice as we trudged through the belt of snow, but I gritted my teeth and walked off the effects of the cold. The worst bit was getting up at dusk, having slept with my feet tucked beneath me all day. There was always an hour or two after waking when my toes tingled and I thought they'd drop off. Then the blood would circulate and everything would be fine — until the next night.

Sleeping outside was dreadfully uncomfortable. The two of us would lie down together in our clothes – which we hadn't changed out of since reaching the snow – and pull rough blankets we'd made from deer skins over our bodies. But even with our shared warmth it was freezing. Madam Octa had it easy — she slept safe and snug in her cage, only waking to feed every few days. I often wished I could change places with her.

If the Little People felt the cold, they gave no indication. They didn't bother with blankets, just lay down beneath a bush or against a rock when they wanted to sleep.

Almost three weeks after we'd last stopped at a way-station, we came to another. I couldn't wait to sit beside a fire and eat cooked meat again. I was even looking forward to sleeping in a coffin — anything was better than hard, cold earth! This way-station was a cave set low in a cliff, above a forest ring and a large stream. Mr Crepsley and me aimed directly for it — a strong moon in the clear night sky lit the way — while the Little People went off to hunt. The climb only took ten minutes. I pushed ahead of Mr Crepsley as we approached the mouth of the cave, eager to get the fire started, only for him to lay a hand on my shoulder. "Hold," he said softly.

"What?" I snapped. I was irritable after three weeks of sleeping rough.

"I smell blood," he said.

Pausing, I sniffed the air, and after a few seconds I got the whiff too, strong and sickly.

"Stay close behind me," Mr Crepsley whispered. "Be prepared to run the instant I give the order." I nodded obediently, then trailed after him as he crept to the opening and slid inside.

The cave was dark, especially after the brightness of the moonlit night, and we entered slowly, giving our eyes time to adjust. It was a deep cave, turning off to the left and going back twenty or more metres. Three coffins had been placed on stands in the middle, but one was lying on the floor, its lid hanging off, and another had been smashed to pieces against the wall to our right.

The wall and floor around the shattered coffin were dark with blood. It wasn't fresh, but by its smell it wasn't more than a couple of nights old. Having checked the rest of the cave — to ensure we were alone — Mr Crepsley edged over to the blood and crouched to examine it, dipping a finger into the dried pool, then tasting it.

"*Well?*" I hissed, as he stood, rubbing his finger and thumb together.

"It is the blood of a vampire," he said quietly.

My insides tightened — I'd been hoping it was the blood of a wild animal. "What do you think—" I started to ask, when there was a sudden rushing sound behind me. A strong arm wrapped around my middle, a thick hand clutched my throat, and — as Mr Crepsley shot forward to help — my attacker grunted triumphantly: "*Hah!*"

CHAPTER FOUR

As I stiffened helplessly, my life in the hands of whoever had hold of me, Mr Crepsley leapt, the fingers of his right hand outstretched like a blade. He sliced the hand over the top of my head. My assailant released me and ducked in the same movement, dropping heavily to the floor as Mr Crepsley sailed by. As the vampire rolled to his feet and spun to strike a second blow, the man who'd snatched me roared, "Stop, Larten! It's me — Gavner!"

Mr Crepsley paused and I got to my feet, coughing from the fright, but no longer afraid. Turning, I saw a burly man with a scarred, patchy face and dark rims around both his eyes. He was dressed in similar clothes to ours, with a cap pulled down over his ears. I recognized him instantly — Gavner Purl, a Vampire General. I'd met him years ago, shortly before my run-in with Murlough.

"You bloody fool, Gavner!" Mr Crepsley shouted. "I

would have killed you if I had connected! Why did you sneak up on us?"

"I wanted to surprise you," Gavner said. "I've been shadowing you most of the night, and this seemed like the perfect time to close in. I didn't expect to almost lose my head in the process," he grumbled.

"You should have been paying more attention to your surroundings and less to Darren and I," Mr Crepsley said, pointing towards the blood-stained wall and floor.

"By the blood of the vampaneze!" Gavner hissed.

"Actually, it is the blood of a vampire," Mr Crepsley corrected him dryly.

"Any idea whose?" Gavner asked, hurrying over to test the blood.

"None," Mr Crepsley said.

Gavner prowled around the confines of the cave, studying the blood and broken coffin, searching for further clues. Finding none, he returned to where we were standing and scratched his chin thoughtfully. "He was probably attacked by a wild animal," he mused aloud. "A bear – maybe more than one – caught him during the day, while he was sleeping."

"I am not so sure of that," Mr Crepsley disagreed. "A bear would have caused great damage to the cave and its contents, but only the coffins have been disturbed."

Gavner ran his eyes over the cave again, noting the tidy state of the rest of it, and nodded. "What do you think happened?" he asked.

"A fight," Mr Crepsley suggested. "Between two vampires, or between the dead vampire and somebody else."

"Who'd be out here in the middle of nowhere?" I asked.

Mr Crepsley and Gavner exchanged a troubled look. "Vampire hunters, perhaps," Gavner muttered.

My breath caught in my throat — I'd grown so used to the vampire way of life, I'd all but forgotten that there were people in the world who thought we were monsters and made it their business to hunt us down and kill us.

"Or maybe humans who chanced upon him by accident and panicked," Mr Crepsley said. "It has been a long time since vampire hunters aggressively trailed us. This may have been a case of mere misfortune."

"Either way," Gavner said, "let's not hang around and wait for it to happen again. I was looking forward to resting, but now I think it's best we don't cage ourselves in."

"Agreed," Mr Crepsley replied, and after one last sweep of the cave, we retreated, senses alert to the slightest hint of an attack.

*   *   *

We made our base for the night in the middle of a ring of thick trees, and lit a rare fire — all of us felt chilled to the bone after our experience in the cave. While we were discussing the dead vampire and whether we should search the surrounding area for his body, the Little People returned, carrying a young deer they'd captured. They stared suspiciously at Gavner, who stared just as suspiciously back.

"What are *they* doing with you?" he hissed.

"Mr Tiny insisted I bring them," Mr Crepsley said, then raised a quieting hand as Gavner swivelled to ask more questions. "Later," he promised. "Let us eat first and dwell upon the death of our comrade."

The trees sheltered us from the rising sun, so we sat up long after dawn, discussing the dead vampire. Since there wasn't anything we could do about him — the vampires decided against a search, on the grounds that it would slow us down — talk eventually turned to other matters. Gavner asked about the Little People again, and Mr Crepsley told him how Mr Tiny had appeared and sent them with us. Then he asked Gavner why he'd been trailing us.

"I knew you'd be presenting Darren to the Princes," Gavner said, "so I located your mental pattern and traced you through it." (Vampires are able to bond mentally with each other.) "I had to cut up from a hundred miles south, but I hate travelling alone — it's boring having no one to chat with."

As we talked, I noticed a couple of toes were missing from Gavner's left foot and asked about them. "Frostbite," he answered cheerfully, wriggling the three remaining toes. "I broke my leg coming here a couple of Councils back. Had to crawl for five nights to reach a way-station. It was only by the luck of the vampires that I didn't lose more than a few toes."

The vampires talked a lot about the past, old friends and previous Councils. I thought they'd mention Murlough — Gavner had alerted Mr Crepsley to the mad vampaneze's whereabouts — but they didn't, not even in passing.

"How have *you* been?" Gavner asked me.

"Fine," I said.

"Life with this sour buzzard hasn't got you down?"

"I've coped so far," I smiled.

"Any intentions of topping up?" he asked.

"Pardon?"

He raised his fingers so I could see the ten scars on the tips, the usual sign of a vampire. "Do you plan to become a full-vampire?"

"No," I said quickly, then looked sideways at Mr Crepsley. "I *don't* have any such plans, do I?" I asked suspiciously.

"No," Mr Crepsley smiled. "Not until you have come of human age. If we made a full-vampire of you now, it would be sixty or seventy years before you were fully grown."

"I bet it's horrible ageing so slowly when you're a kid," Gavner noted.

"It is," I sighed.

"Things will improve with time," Mr Crepsley said.

"Sure," I said sarcastically, "when I'm all grown up — thirty years from now!" I rose and shook my head, disgusted. I often got downhearted when my thoughts turned to the decades I'd have to spend on the road to maturity.

"Where are you going?" Mr Crepsley asked as I headed towards the trees.

"To the stream," I said, "to fill our canteens."

"Maybe one of us should go with you," Gavner said.

"Darren is not a child," Mr Crepsley answered before I could. "He will be fine."

I hid a grin — I enjoyed the rare occasions when the vampire passed a compliment about me — and continued down to the stream. The chilly water was fast-flowing and gurgled loudly as I filled the canteens, splashing around the rims and my fingers. If I'd been human I might have got frostbite, but vampires are a lot sturdier.

As I was corking the second canteen, a tiny cloud of steamy breath drifted across from the other side of the stream. I glanced up, surprised that a wild animal had ventured this close, and found myself staring into the flaming eyes of a fierce, hungry-looking, sharp-fanged wolf.

CHAPTER FIVE

THE WOLF studied me silently, its nose crinkling over its jagged canines as it sniffed my scent. I gently laid my canteen aside, not sure what to do. If I called for help, the wolf might panic and flee — then again, it might attack. If I stayed as I was, it might lose interest and slink away — or it might take it as a sign of weakness and move in for the kill.

I was desperately trying to decide when the wolf tensed its hind legs, lowered its head and pounced, crossing the stream with one mighty bound. It crashed into my chest, knocking me to the ground. I tried scrambling away but the wolf had perched on top of me and was too heavy to throw off. My hands searched frantically for a rock or stick, something to beat the animal with, but there was nothing to grab except snow.

The wolf was a terrifying sight up close, with its dark grey face and slanting yellow eyes, its black muzzle and bared white teeth, some five or six centimetres long. Its tongue lolled out the side of its mouth and it was panting slowly. Its breath stank of blood and raw animal flesh.

I knew nothing about wolves – except vampires couldn't drink from them – so I didn't know how to react: attack its face or go for its body? Lie still and hope it went away, or shout and maybe scare it off? While my brain was spinning, the wolf lowered its head, extended its long wet tongue, and ...*licked me!*

I was so stunned, I just lay there, staring up at the jaws of the fearsome animal. The wolf licked me again, then got off, faced the stream, went down on its paws and lapped at the water. I lay where I was a few moments more, then pulled myself up and sat watching it drink, noting that it was a male.

When the wolf had drunk his fill, he stood, lifted his head and howled. From the trees on the opposite side of the stream, three more wolves emerged and crept down to the bank, where they drank. Two were females and one was a young cub, darker and smaller than the others.

The male watched the others drinking, then sat beside me. He snuggled up to me like a dog and, before I knew what I was doing, I'd reached around and was tickling him behind his ear. The wolf whined pleasantly and cocked his head so I could scratch behind the other ear.

One of the she-wolves finished drinking and jumped the stream. She sniffed my feet, then sat on the other side of me and offered her head to be scratched. The male growled at her jealously but she took no notice.

The other two weren't long joining the couple on my side of the stream. The female was shyer than her mates and hovered several metres away. The cub had no such fears and crawled over my legs and belly, sniffing like a hound-dog. He cocked a leg to mark my left thigh, but before he could, the male wolf snapped at him and sent him tumbling. He barked angrily, then slunk back and climbed over me again. This time he didn't try to mark his territory — thankfully!

I sat there for ages, playing with the cub and tickling the bigger pair of wolves. The male rolled over on to his back, so that I could rub his belly. His hair was lighter underneath, except for a long streak of black hair which ran part-way up his middle. 'Streak' seemed like a good name for a wolf, so that's what I called him.

I wanted to see if they knew any tricks, so I found a stick and threw it. "Fetch, Streak, fetch!" I shouted, but he didn't budge. I tried getting him to sit to attention. "Sit, Streak!" I ordered. He stared at me. "Sit — like this." I squatted on my haunches. Streak moved back a little, as though he thought I might be mad. The cub was delighted and jumped on me. I laughed and stopped trying to teach them tricks.

After that I headed back to camp to tell the vampires about my new friends. The wolves followed, though only Streak walked by my side — the others trailed behind.

Mr Crepsley and Gavner were asleep when I got back, tucked beneath thick deer blankets. Gavner was snoring loudly. With only their heads showing, they looked like the ugliest pair of babies in the world! I wished I had a camera capable of photographing vampires, so that I could snap them.

I was about to join them beneath the blankets when I had an idea. The wolves had stopped at the trees. I coaxed them in. Streak came first and examined the copse, making sure it was safe. When he was satisfied, he growled lightly and the other wolves entered, keeping away from the sleeping vampires.

I lay down on the far side of the fire and held a blanket up, inviting the wolves to lie down with me. They wouldn't go beneath the blanket – the cub tried, but its mother jerked it back by the scruff of its neck – but once I lay down and covered myself with it, they crept up and lay on top, even the shy she-wolf. They were heavy, and the scent of their hairy bodies was overbearing, but the warmth of the wolves was heavenly, and despite the fact that I was resting so close to the cave where a vampire had been killed recently, I slept in complete comfort.

* * *

I was awakened by angry growls. Jolting upright, I found the three adult wolves spread in a semicircle in front of my bed, the male in the middle. The cub was cowering behind me. Ahead stood the Little People. Their grey hands were flexing by their sides and they were moving in on the wolves.

"Stop!" I roared, leaping to my feet. On the other side of the fire – which had died out while I was sleeping – Mr Crepsley and Gavner snapped awake and rolled out from under their blankets. I jumped in front of Streak and snarled at the Little People. They stared at me from beneath their blue hoods. I glimpsed the large green eyes of the one closest me.

"What's happening?" Gavner shouted, blinking rapidly.

The nearest Little Person ignored Gavner, pointed at the wolves, then at his belly, and rubbed it. That was the sign that he was hungry. I shook my head. "Not the wolves," I told him. "They're my friends." He made the rubbing motion again. "No!" I shouted.

The Little Person began to advance, but the one behind him — Lefty — reached out and touched his arm. The Little Person locked gazes with Lefty, stood still a moment, then shuffled away to where he'd left the rats they'd caught while hunting. Lefty lingered a moment, his hidden green eyes on mine, before joining his brother (I always thought of them as brothers).

"I see you have met some of our cousins," Mr Crepsley said, stepping slowly over the remains of the fire, holding his hands palms-up so the wolves wouldn't be alarmed. They growled at him, but once they caught his scent they relaxed and sat, though they kept a wary eye on the munching Little People.

"*Cousins?*" I asked.

"Wolves and vampires are related," he explained. "Legends claim that once we were the same, just as man and ape were originally one. Some of us learned to walk on two legs and became vampires — the others remained wolves."

"Is that true?" I asked.

Mr Crepsley shrugged. "Where legends are concerned, who knows?" He crouched in front of Streak and studied him silently. Streak sat up straight and ruffled his head to make his ears and mane erect. "A fine specimen," Mr Crepsley said, stroking the wolf's long snout. "A born leader."

"I call him Streak, because he's got a streak of black hair on his belly," I said.

"Wolves have no need of names," the vampire informed me. "They are not dogs."

"Don't be a spoilsport," Gavner said, stepping up beside his friend. "Let him give them names if he wants. It can't do any harm."

"I suppose not," Mr Crepsley agreed. He held out a hand to the she-wolves and they stepped forward to lick his palm, including the shy one. "I always had a way with wolves," he said, unable to keep the pride out of his voice.

"How come they're so friendly?" I asked. "I thought wolves shied away from people."

"From humans," Mr Crepsley said. "Vampires are different. Our scent is similar to their own. They recognize us as kindred spirits. Not all wolves are amiable – these must have had dealings with our kind before – but none would ever attack a vampire, not unless they were starving."

"Did you see any more of them?" Gavner asked. I shook my head. "Then they're probably journeying towards Vampire Mountain to join up with other packs."

"Why would they be going to Vampire Mountain?" I asked.

"Wolves come whenever there's a Council," he explained. "They know from experience that there will be plenty of scraps for them to feed on. The guardians of Vampire Mountain spend years stocking up for Councils. There's always food left over, which they dump outside for the creatures of the wild to dispose of."

"It's a long way to go for a few scraps," I commented.

"They go for more than food," Mr Crepsley said. "They gather for company, to salute old friends, find new mates and share memories."

"Wolves can communicate?" I asked.

"They are able to transmit simple thoughts to one another. They do not actually talk – wolves have no words – but can share pictures and pass on maps of where they have been, letting others know where hunting is plentiful or scarce."

"Talking of which, we'd better make *ourselves* scarce," Gavner said. "The sun's sinking and it's time we got a move on. You chose a long, roundabout route to come by, Larten, and if we don't pick up the pace, we'll arrive late for Council."

"There are other paths?" I asked.

"Of course," he said. "There are dozens of ways. That's why – except for the remains of the dead one – we haven't run into other vampires — each comes by a different route."

We rolled up our blankets and departed, Mr Crepsley and Gavner keeping a close eye on the trail, scouring it for signs of whoever had killed the vampire in the cave. The wolves followed us through the trees and ran beside us for a couple of hours, keeping clear of the Little People, before vanishing ahead of us into the night.

"Where are they going?" I asked.

"To hunt," Mr Crepsley replied.

"Will they come back?"

"It would not surprise me," he said, and, come dawn, as we were making camp, the four wolves re-appeared like ghosts out of the snow and made their beds beside and on top of us. For the second day running, I slept soundly, disturbed only by the cold nose of the cub when he snuck in under the blanket during the middle of the day to cuddle up beside me.

CHAPTER SIX

WE PROCEEDED with caution for the first few nights after finding the blood-spattered cave. But when we encountered no further signs of the vampire killer, we put our concerns on hold and enjoyed the rough pleasures of the trail as best we could.

Running with wolves was fascinating. I learnt lots by watching them and asking questions of Mr Crepsley, who fancied himself something of a wolf expert.

Wolves aren't fast, but they're tireless, sometimes roaming forty or fifty kilometres a day. They usually pick on small animals when hunting, but occasionally go after larger victims, working as a team. Their senses — sight, hearing, smell — are strong. Each pack has a leader, and they share food equally. They're great climbers, able to survive any sort of conditions.

We hunted with them often. It was exhilarating to race alongside them on bright star-speckled nights, over the gleaming snow — chasing a deer or fox and sharing the hot, bloody kill. Time passed quicker with the wolves around, and the kilometres slipped by almost unnoticed.

*   *   *

One cold, clear night, we came upon a thick briar patch which covered the floor of a valley sheltered between two towering mountains. The thorns were extra thick and sharp, capable of pricking the skin of even a full-vampire. We paused at the mouth of the valley while Mr Crepsley and Gavner decided how to proceed.

"We could climb the side of one of the mountains," Mr Crepsley mused, "but Darren is not as strong a climber as us — he could be damaged if he slipped."

"How about going around?" Gavner suggested.

"It would take too long."

"Could we dig a way under?" I asked.

"Again," Mr Crepsley said, "it would take too long. We will just have to pick our way through as carefully as we can."

He removed his jumper and so did Gavner.

"What are you getting undressed for?" I asked.

"Our clothes would protect us a bit," Gavner explained, "but we'd come out the other end in tattered rags. Best to keep them intact."

When Gavner took off his trousers, we saw he was wearing a pair of yellow boxer shorts with pink elephants stitched into them. Mr Crepsley stared at the shorts incredulously. "They were a present," Gavner mumbled, blushing furiously.

"From a human female you were romantically involved with, I presume," Mr Crepsley said, the corners of his normally stern mouth twitching upwards, threatening to split into a rare unrestrained smile.

"She was a lovely woman," Gavner sighed, tracing the outline of one of the elephants. "She just had very poor taste in underwear..."

"And in boyfriends," I added impishly. Mr Crepsley burst into laughter at that and doubled over, tears streaming down his face. I'd never seen the vampire laugh so much – I'd never guessed he could! Even Gavner looked surprised.

It took Mr Crepsley a long time to recover from his laughing fit. When he'd wiped the tears away and was back to his normal sombre self, he apologized (as though laughing were a crime). He then rubbed some foul-smelling lotion into my skin, which sealed the pores, making it harder to cut. Without wasting any more time, we advanced. The going was slow and painful. No matter how careful I was, every few metres I'd step on a thorn or scratch myself. I protected my face as best I could, but by the time we were halfway into the valley, my cheeks were specked with shallow red rivulets.

The Little People hadn't removed their blue robes, even though the cloth was being cut to ribbons. After a while, Mr Crepsley told them to walk in front, so they endured the worst of the thorns while beating a path for the rest of us. I almost felt sorry for the silent, uncomplaining pair.

The wolves had the easiest time. They were built for terrain like this, and slinked through the briars swiftly. But they weren't happy. They'd been acting strangely all night, creeping along beside us, low of spirit, sniffing the air suspiciously. We could sense their anxiety, but didn't know what was causing it.

I was watching my feet, stepping carefully over a row of glinting thorns, when I ran into Mr Crepsley, who'd come to a sudden stop. "What's up?" I asked, peering over his shoulder.

"Gavner!" he snapped, ignoring my question.

Gavner shuffled past me, breathing heavily (we often teased him about his heavy breathing). I heard him utter a choked cry as he reached Mr Crepsley.

"What is it?" I asked. "Let me see." The vampires parted and I saw a tiny piece of cloth snagged on a briar bush. A few drops of dried blood had stained the tips of the thorns.

"What's the big deal?" I asked.

The vampires didn't answer immediately — they were gazing around worriedly, much the same way that the wolves were.

"Can't you smell it?" Gavner finally replied quietly.

"What?"

"The blood."

I sniffed the air. There was only the faintest of scents because the blood was dry. "What about it?" I asked.

"Think back six years," Mr Crepsley said. He picked the cloth off the briar — the wolves were growling loudly now — and thrust it under my nostrils. "Breathe deeply. Ring any bells?"

It didn't straightaway — my senses weren't as sharp as a full-vampire's — but then I recalled that long-ago night in

Debbie Hemlock's bedroom, and the smell of the insane Murlough's blood as he lay dying on the floor. My face turned white as I realized — it was the blood of a *vampaneze!*

CHAPTER SEVEN

WE MADE quick time through the remainder of the briar patch, taking no notice of the cutting thorns. On the far side we stopped to get dressed, then hurried on without pause. There was a way-station nearby that Mr Crepsley was determined to reach before the break of day. The journey would normally have taken several hours but we made it in two. Once inside and secure, the vampires fell into a heated discussion. They'd never encountered evidence of vampaneze activity in this part of the world before — there was a treaty between the two clans, preventing such acts of trespass.

"Maybe it's a mad wanderer," Gavner suggested.

"Even the most insane vampaneze knows better than to come here," Mr Crepsley disagreed.

"What other explanation could there be?" Gavner asked.

Mr Crepsley considered the problem. "He could be a spy."

"You think the vampaneze would risk war?" Gavner sounded dubious. "What could they learn that would justify such a gamble?"

"Maybe it's *us* they're after," I said quietly. I didn't want to interrupt but felt I had to.

"What do you mean?" Gavner asked.

"Maybe they found out about Murlough."

Gavner's face paled and Mr Crepsley's eyes narrowed. "How could they have?" he snapped.

"Mr Tiny knew," I reminded him.

"Mr Tiny knows about Murlough?" Gavner hissed.

Mr Crepsley nodded slowly. "But even if he had told the vampaneze, how would they know we were coming *this* way? We could have chosen any number of paths. They could not have second-guessed us."

"Perhaps they're covering all the paths," Gavner said.

"No," Mr Crepsley said confidently. "It is too far-fetched. Whatever the vampaneze's reason for being here, I am sure it has nothing to do with *us*."

"I hope you're right," Gavner grumbled, unconvinced.

We discussed it some more, including the question of whether the vampaneze had killed the vampire in the previous way-station, then grabbed a few hours of shut-eye, taking turns to remain on watch. I barely slept as I was worrying about being attacked by the purple-faced killers.

When night came, Mr Crepsley said we should progress no further until we were sure the way was safe. "We cannot risk running into a pack of vampaneze," he said. "We will scout the area, make sure we are not in danger, then carry on as before."

"Have we time to go scouting?" Gavner asked.

"We must make time," Mr Crepsley insisted. "Better to waste a few nights than run into a trap."

I stayed in the cave while they went scouting. I didn't want to – I kept thinking about what had happened to that other vampire – but they said I'd be in the way if I came — a vampaneze would hear me coming a hundred metres away.

The Little People, she-wolves and cub stayed with me. Streak went with the vampires — the wolves had sensed the vampaneze presence before we did, so it would be helpful for them to have one along.

It was lonely without the vampires and Streak. The Little People were aloof as always – they spent a lot of the day stitching their blue robes back into shape – and the she-wolves lay out and snoozed. Only the cub provided me with company. We spent hours playing together, in the cave and among the trees of a nearby small forest. I'd called the cub Rudi, after Rudolf the red-nosed reindeer, because of his fondness for rubbing his cold nose into my back while I was asleep.

I caught a couple of squirrels in the forest and cooked them, so they were ready in the morning when the vampires returned. I served hot berries and roots with them — Mr Crepsley had taught me which wild foods were safe to eat. Gavner thanked me for the food but Mr Crepsley was distant and didn't say much. They'd discovered no further trace of the vampaneze, and that worried them — a mad vampaneze couldn't have covered his tracks so expertly. That meant we were dealing with one – or more – in full control of his senses.

Gavner wanted to flit ahead to consult with the other vampires, but Mr Crepsley wouldn't let him — the laws against flitting on the way to Vampire Mountain were more important than our safety, he insisted.

It was strange how Gavner went along with most of what Mr Crepsley said. As a General, he could have ordered us to do whatever he pleased. But I'd never seen him pull rank on Mr Crepsley. Maybe it was because Mr Crepsley had once been a General of high ranking. He'd been on the verge of becoming a Vampire Prince when he quit. Perhaps Gavner still considered Mr Crepsley his superior.

After a full day's sleep, the vampires set off to scout the land ahead again. If the way was clear, we'd start back on the trail to Vampire Mountain the next night.

I ate a simple breakfast, then Rudi and me headed down to the forest to play. Rudi loved being away from the adult wolves. He was able to explore freely, with no one to snap at him or cuff him round the head if he misbehaved. He tried climbing trees but was too short for most. Finally he found one with low-hanging branches and he clambered halfway up. Once there, he looked down and whimpered.

"Come on," I laughed. "You're not *that* high up. There's no need to be afraid." He ignored me and went on whimpering. Then he bared his fangs and growled.

I stepped closer, puzzled by his behaviour. "What's wrong?" I asked. "Are you stuck? Do you want help?" The cub yapped. He sounded genuinely frightened. "OK, Rudi," I said, "I'm coming up to—"

I was silenced by a bone-shattering roar. Turning, I saw a huge dark bear lurching over the top of a snow-drift. It landed heavily, shook its snout, snarled, fixed its gaze upon me — then lunged, teeth flashing, claws exposed, intent on cutting me down!

CHAPTER EIGHT

THE BEAR would have killed me, if not for Rudi. The cub leapt from the tree, landing on top of the bear's head, momentarily blinding it. The bear roared and swiped at the cub, who ducked and bit one of its ears. The bear roared again and shook its head viciously from side to side. Rudi held on for a couple of seconds, before he was sent flying into a thicket.

The bear resumed its attack on me, but in the time the cub had bought, I'd ducked round the tree and was racing for the cave as fast as I could. The bear lurched after me, realized I was too far ahead, bellowed angrily, turned and went looking for Rudi.

I stopped when I heard frightened yapping. Glancing over my shoulder, I saw that the cub had made it back up the tree, the bark of which the bear was now ripping to pieces with its claws. Rudi was in no immediate danger, but sooner or later he'd slip or the bear would shake him down, and that would be the end of him.

I paused no more than a second, then turned, picked up a rock and the thickest stick I could find, and sped back to try and save Rudi.

The bear let go of the tree when it saw me coming, dropped to its haunches and met my challenge. It was a huge beast, maybe a metre and a half high; it had black fur, a white quarter-moon mark across its chest and a whitish face. Foam flecked its jaws and its eyes were wild, as though touched by rabid madness.

I stopped in front of the bear and whacked the ground with my stick. "Come on, Grizzly," I growled. It snarled and tossed its head. I glanced up at Rudi, hoping he'd have enough sense to slink down the tree and retreat to the cave, but he stayed where he was, petrified, unable to let go.

The bear swiped at me but I ducked out of the way of its massive paw. Rearing up on its hind legs, it collapsed flat upon me, trying to crush me with the weight of its body. I avoided it again, but it was a closer call this time.

I was prodding at the bear's face with the end of the stick, aiming for its eyes, when the she-wolves rushed on to the scene — they must have heard Rudi's yapping. The bear howled as one of the wolves leapt and bit deep into its shoulder, while the other attached herself to its legs, tearing at them with her teeth and claws. It shook off the uppermost wolf and bent to deal with the lower one, which was when I darted in with my stick and jabbed at its left ear.

I must have hurt it, because it lost interest in the wolves and hurled itself at me. I ducked out of the way of its body but one of its burly forelegs connected with the side of my head and knocked me to the ground.

The bear rolled to its feet and made for me, scattering the wolves with swipes of its claws. I scrabbled backwards, but not fast enough. Suddenly the bear was above me, standing erect, bellowing triumphantly — it had me exactly where it wanted! I slammed the stick against its stomach, then the rock, but it took no notice of such feeble blows. Leering, it started to fall...

...which was when the Little People barrelled into its back and knocked it off balance. Their timing couldn't have been any sweeter.

The bear must have thought the entire world was conspiring against it. Every time it had me in its sights, something new got in the way. Roaring loudly at the Little People, it threw itself at them madly. The one with the limp stepped out of its way but the other got trapped beneath it.

The Little Person raised his short arms, jammed them against the bear's torso and tried to shove it aside. The Little Person was strong, but he stood no chance against such a massive foe, and the bear came crashing down and flattened him. There was a horrible crunching sound and when the bear got to its feet, I saw the Little Person lying in pieces, broken bones jutting out of his body at crooked green angles.

The bear lifted its head and bellowed at the sky, then fixed its eyes on me and leered hungrily. Dropping to all fours, it advanced. The wolves leapt at it but it shook them loose as though they were fleas. I was still dazed from the blow, not able to get to my feet. I began crawling through the snow.

As the bear closed in for the kill, the second Little Person – the one I called Lefty – stepped in front of it, caught it by its ears, and *head-butted* it! It was the craziest thing I'd ever seen, but it did a remarkably effective job. The bear grunted and blinked dumbly. Lefty head-butted it again and was rearing his head back for a third blow when the bear struck at him with its right paw, like a boxer.

It hit Lefty in the chest and knocked him down. His hood had fallen off during the struggle and I could see his grey stitched-together face and round green eyes. There was a mask over his mouth, like the sort doctors wear during surgery. He stared up at the bear, unafraid, waiting for the killer blow.

"No!" I screamed. Stumbling to my knees, I threw a punch at the bear. It snarled at me. I punched it again, then grabbed a handful of snow and threw it into the beast's eyes.

While the bear cleared its vision, I looked for a weapon. I was desperate — anything was better than my bare hands. At first I saw nothing I could use, but then my eyes fell on the bones sticking out of the dead Little Person's body. Acting on instinct, I rolled across to where the Little Person lay, took hold of one of the longer bones, and pulled. It was covered in blood and my fingers slipped off. Trying again, I got a firmer hold and worked it from side to side. After a few tugs it snapped near the base and suddenly I wasn't defenceless any longer.

The bear had regained its sight and was pounding towards me. Lefty was still on the ground. The wolves were barking furiously, unable to do anything to deter the charging bear. The cub yapped from its perch in the tree.

I was on my own. Me against the bear. No one could help me now.

Spinning, using all my extra-sharp vampire abilities, I rolled beneath the clutching claws of the bear, jumped to my feet, picked my spot, and rammed the tip of the bone deep into the bear's unprotected neck.

The bear came to a halt. Its eyes bulged. Its forelegs dropped by its sides. For a moment it stood, gasping painfully, the bone sticking out of its neck. Then it crashed to the ground, shook horribly for a few seconds — and died.

I fell on top of the dead bear and lay there. I was shaking and crying, more from fright than pain. I'd looked death in the eye before, but never had I been involved in a fight as savage as this.

Eventually, one of the she-wolves — the normally shy one — cuddled up to me and licked around my face, making sure I was all right. I patted her to show I was OK, and buried my face in her neck, drying my tears on her hair. When I felt able, I stood and gazed at the area around me.

The other she-wolf was by the tree, coaxing Rudi down — the cub was even more shaken than me. The dead Little Person lay not far away, his blood seeping into the snow, turning it crimson. Lefty was sitting up, checking himself for injuries.

I made my way over to Lefty to thank him for saving my life. He was incredibly ugly without his hood: he had grey skin, and his face was a mass of scars and stitches. He had no ears or nose that I could see, and his round green eyes were set near the top of his head, not in the middle of his face like they are with most people. He was completely hairless.

Any other time I might have been frightened, but this creature had risked his life to save mine, and all I felt was gratitude. "Are you OK, Lefty?" I asked. He looked up and nodded. "That was a close call," I half-laughed. Again he nodded. "Thanks for coming to my rescue. I'd have been a goner if you hadn't stepped in." I sank to the ground beside him and gazed at the bear, then at the dead Little Person. "Sorry about your partner, Lefty," I said softly. "Shall we bury him?"

The Little Person shook his large head, started to rise, then paused. He stared into my eyes and I stared back questioningly. By the expression on his face, I almost expected him to speak.

Reaching up, Lefty gently tugged down the mask which covered the lower half of his face. He had a wide mouth full of sharp, yellow teeth. He stuck out his tongue – which was a strange grey colour, like his skin – and licked his lips. When they were wet, he flexed and stretched them a few times, then did the one thing I was sure the Little People could never do. In a creaky, slow, mechanical tone — he *spoke*.

"Name ... not Lefty. Name ... Harkat ... Harkat Mulds." And his lips spread into a jagged gash which was as close to a smile as he could come.

CHAPTER NINE

MR CREPSLEY, Gavner and Streak had been checking a maze of cliff-top tunnels when they heard faint echoes of the fight. They raced back, arriving fifteen minutes or so after I'd killed the bear. They were stunned when I explained what had happened and told them about Harkat Mulds. The Little Person had replaced his robes and hood, and when they asked him if it was true that he could talk, there was a long moment of silence during which I thought he wasn't going to say anything. Then he nodded and croaked, "Yes."

Gavner actually jumped back a few steps when he heard the Little Person speak. Mr Crepsley shook his head, amazed. "We will discuss this later," he said. "First there is the bear to deal with." He crouched beside the dead bear and studied it from top to bottom. "Describe how it attacked you," he said, and I told of the bear's sudden appearance and savage attack. "It makes no sense," Mr Crepsley frowned. "Bears do not behave in such a fashion unless agitated or starving. It was not hunger which motivated it – look at its round stomach – and if you did nothing to upset it..."

"It was foaming at the mouth," I said. "I think it had rabies."

"We shall soon see." The vampire used his sharp nails to cut open the bear's belly. He stuck his nose close to the cut and sniffed the blood that was oozing out. After a few seconds he pulled a face and stood up.

"Well?" Gavner asked.

"The bear *was* mad," Mr Crepsley said, "but not with rabies — it had consumed the blood of a vampaneze!"

"How?" I gasped.

"I am not sure," Mr Crepsley replied, then glanced up at the sky. "We have time before dawn. We will trace this bear's trail and perhaps learn more along the way."

"What about the dead Little Person?" Gavner asked. "Should we bury him?"

"Do you want to bury him ... *Harkat*?" Mr Crepsley asked, echoing my earlier question.

Harkat Mulds shook his head. "Not really."

"Then leave him," the vampire snapped. "Scavengers and birds will pick his bones clean. We do not have time to waste."

The path of the bear was easy to follow — even an untrained tracker like me could have traced it by the deep footprints and broken twigs.

Night was drawing to a close as we pulled up at a small mound of stones and found what had driven the bear mad.

Half-buried beneath the stones was a purple body with a red head of hair — a vampaneze!

"By the way his skull is crushed, he must have died in a fall," Mr Crepsley said, examining the dead man. "The bear found him after he was buried and dug him up. See the chunks that have been bitten out of him?" He pointed to the gaping holes in the vampaneze's belly. "That is what drove it mad — the blood of vampaneze and vampires is poisonous. Had you not killed it, it would have died in another night or two anyway."

"So that's where our mystery vampaneze was," Gavner grunted. "No wonder we couldn't find him."

"We don't have to worry about him any more, do we?" I sighed happily.

"Quite the contrary," Mr Crepsley snapped. "We have more reason to worry now than before."

"Why?" I asked. "He's dead, isn't he?"

"He is," Mr Crepsley agreed, then pointed to the stones which had been laid over the vampaneze. *"But who buried him?"*

* * *

We made camp at the base of a cliff, using branches and leaves to create a shelter where the vampires could sleep, safe from the sun. Once they were inside, Harkat and me sat by the entrance and the Little Person told his incredible story. The wolves had gone off hunting, except for Rudi, who curled up in my lap and dozed.

"My memories ... are not ... complete," said Harkat.

Speaking wasn't easy for him and he had to pause for breath often. "Much is ... clouded. I will tell ... you what ... I remember. First — I am a ... ghost."

Our jaws dropped.

"A ghost!" Mr Crepsley shouted. "Absurd!"

"Absolutely," Gavner agreed with a grin. "Vampires don't believe in crazy things like ghosts, do we, Larten?"

Before Mr Crepsley could reply, Harkat corrected himself. "What I should ... have said ... is, I ... *was* a ghost. All ... Little People ... were ghosts. Until ... they agreed terms ... with Mr Tiny."

"I don't understand," Gavner said. "Agree what terms? How?"

"Mr Tiny can ... talk with ... dead," Harkat explained. "I did not ... leave Earth ... when I died. Soul ... could not. I was ... stuck. Mr Tiny found ... me. Said he'd give ... me a ... body, so I ... could live again. In return ... I'd serve him, as a ... Little Person."

According to Harkat, each of the Little People had struck a deal with Mr Tiny, and each deal was different. They didn't have to serve him forever. Sooner or later, they would be freed, some to live on in their grey, short bodies, some to be reborn, others to move on to Heaven or Paradise or wherever it is that dead souls go.

"Mr Tiny has that much power?" Mr Crepsley asked.

Harkat nodded.

"What deal did *you* strike with him?" I asked curiously.

"I do not ... know," he said. "I cannot ... remember."

There were lots of things he couldn't remember. He didn't know who he'd been when he was alive, when or where he'd lived, or how long he'd been dead. He didn't even know if he'd been a man or a woman! The Little People were genderless, which meant they were neither male nor female.

"So how do we refer to you?" Gavner asked. "He? She? It?"

"*He* will ... do fine," Harkat said.

Their blue robes and hoods were for show. Their masks, on the other hand, were necessary, and they carried several spares, some stitched under their skin for extra safe-keeping! Air was lethal to them — if they breathed normal air for ten or twelve hours, they'd die. There were chemicals in their masks which purified the air.

"How can you die if you're already dead?" I asked, confused.

"My body can ... die, like anyone ... else's. If it does ... my soul goes ... back to the way ... it was."

"Could you agree another contract with Mr Tiny?" Mr Crepsley asked.

Harkat shook his head. "Not sure. But don't ... think so. One shot at ... extra life is ... all I think ... we get."

The Little People could read each other's minds. That's why they never spoke. He wasn't sure if the others were able to speak or not. When asked why he'd never spoken before, he pulled a crooked grin and said he'd never had cause to.

"But there must be a reason," Mr Crepsley pressed. "In all the hundreds of years that we have known them, no Little Person has ever spoken, even when dying or in great pain. Why have *you* broken that long silence? And *why?*"

Harkat hesitated. "I have a ... message," he finally said. "Mr Tiny ... gave me it ... to give to ... Vampire Princes. So I'd ... have had to speak ... soon anyway."

"A *message?*" Mr Crepsley leant forward intently, but pulled back into the shadows of the shelter when the sun hit him. "What sort of message?"

"It is for ... Princes," Harkat said. "I do not ... think I should ... tell you."

"Go on, Harkat," I urged him. "We won't tell them you told us. You can trust us."

"You will ... not tell?" he asked Mr Crepsley and Gavner.

"My lips are sealed," Gavner promised.

Mr Crepsley was slower to make his pledge, but finally nodded.

Harkat took a deep, shuddering breath. "Mr Tiny told ... me to tell ... Princes that the ... night of the ... Vampaneze Lord ... is at hand. That is ... all."

"The night of the Vampaneze Lord is at hand?" I repeated. "What kind of a message is that?"

"I do not ... know what ... it means," Harkat said. "I'm just ... the messenger."

"Gavner, do you–" I started to ask, but stopped when I saw the expressions of the vampires. Though Harkat's message meant nothing to me, it obviously meant a great deal to them. Their faces were even paler than usual, and they were trembling with fear. In fact, they couldn't have looked more terrified if they'd been staked to the ground out in the open and left for the sun to rise!

CHAPTER TEN

MR CREPSLEY and Gavner wouldn't explain the meaning of Harkat's message straightaway – they were too stunned to speak – and the story only trickled out over the next three or four nights, most of it coming from Gavner Purl.

It had to do with something Mr Tiny told the vampires hundreds of years ago, when the vampaneze broke away. Once the fighting had died down, he'd visited the Princes at Vampire Mountain and told them that the vampaneze were not hierarchically structured (Mr Crepsley's phrase), which meant there were no Vampaneze Generals or Princes. Nobody gave orders or bossed the others about.

"That was one of the reasons they broke away," Gavner said. "They didn't like the way things worked with vampires. They thought it was unfair that ordinary vampires had to answer to the Generals, and the Generals to the Princes."

Lowering his voice so that Mr Crepsley couldn't hear, he

said, "To be honest, I agree with some of that. There *is* room for change. The vampire system has worked for hundreds of years, but that doesn't mean it's perfect."

"Are you saying you'd rather be a vampaneze?" I asked, shocked.

"Of course not!" he laughed. "They kill, and allow mad vampaneze like Murlough to run around and do as they please. It's far better to be a vampire. But that doesn't mean that *some* of their ideas aren't worth taking on board.

"Not flitting on the way to Vampire Mountain, for example — that's a ridiculous rule, but it can only be changed by the Princes, who don't have to change anything they don't want to, regardless of what the rest of us think. Generals have to do everything the Princes say, and ordinary vampires have to do everything Generals say."

Though the vampaneze didn't believe in leaders, Mr Tiny said that one night a champion would step forward. He would be known as the Vampaneze Lord and the vampaneze would follow him blindly and do everything he said.

"What's so bad about that?" I asked.

"Wait till you hear the next bit," Gavner said gravely. Apparently, not long after the Vampaneze Lord came to power, he would lead the vampaneze into war against the vampires. It was a war, Mr Tiny warned, that the vampires couldn't win. They would be wiped out.

"Is that true?" I asked, appalled.

Gavner shrugged. "We've been asking ourselves that for seven hundred years. Nobody doubts Mr Tiny's powers — he's proved before that he can see into the future — but sometimes he tells lies. He's an evil little worm."

"Why didn't you go after the vampaneze and kill them all?" I asked.

"Mr Tiny said that some vampaneze would survive, and the Vampaneze Lord would come as promised. Besides, war with the vampaneze was exacting too heavy a toll. Humans were hunting us down and might have made an end of us. It was best to declare a truce and let matters lie."

"Is there no way the vampires could beat the vampaneze?" I asked.

"I'm not sure," Gavner replied, scratching his head. "There are more vampires than vampaneze, and we're as strong as they are, so I can't see why we shouldn't be able to get the better of them. But Mr Tiny said numbers wouldn't matter.

"There's one hope," he added. "The Stone of Blood."

"What's that?"

"You'll see when we get to Vampire Mountain. It's a magic icon, sacred to us. Mr Tiny said that if we prevented it from falling into the hands of the vampaneze, one night, long after the battle has been fought and lost, there's a chance that vampires might rise from the ashes and prosper again."

"How?" I asked, frowning.

Gavner smiled. "*That* question has puzzled vampires for as long as it's been asked. Let me know if you figure it out," he said with a wink, and drew the conversation to a troubling close.

*　*　*

A week later, we arrived at Vampire Mountain.

It wasn't the highest mountain in the region, but it was steep and rocky, and looked like it would be almost impossible to climb. "Where's the palace?" I asked, squinting up at the snowy peak, which seemed to point directly at the three-quarter moon overhead.

"Palace?" Mr Crepsley replied.

"Where the Vampire Princes live." Mr Crepsley and Gavner burst out laughing. "What's so funny?" I snapped.

"How long do you think we would escape detection if we built a palace on the side of a mountain?" Mr Crepsley asked.

"Then where...?" Understanding dawned. "It's *inside* the mountain!"

"Of course," Gavner smiled. "The mountain's a giant hive of caves and chambers. Everything a vampire could wish for is stored within — coffins, vats of human blood, food and wine. The only time you see vampires on the outside is when they're arriving or departing or going to hunt."

"How do we get in?" I asked.

Mr Crepsley tapped the side of his nose. "Watch and see."

We walked around the rocky base of the mountain. Mr Crepsley and Gavner were full of excitement, though only Gavner let it show — the older vampire acted as dryly as ever, and it was only when he thought nobody was looking that he'd grin to himself and rub his hands together in anticipation.

We reached a stream which was six or seven metres wide. The water flowed swiftly through it and gushed away down to the flat plains beyond. While we were working our way upstream, a lone wolf appeared in the near distance and howled. Streak and the other wolves came to an immediate stop. Streak's ears pricked up, he listened a moment, then howled back. His tail was wagging when he looked at me.

"He is saying goodbye," Mr Crepsley informed me, but I'd guessed that already.

"Do they have to go?" I asked.

"This is what they came for — to meet others of their kind. It would be cruel to ask them to stay with us."

I nodded glumly and reached down to scratch Streak's ears. "Nice knowing you, Streak," I said. Then I patted Rudi. "I'll miss you, you miserable little runt."

The adult wolves started away. Rudi hesitated, looking from me to the departing wolves. For a second I thought he might choose to stick with me, but then he barked, rubbed his wet nose over the tops of my bare feet, and set off after the others.

"You'll see him again," Gavner promised. "We'll look them up when we leave."

"Sure," I sniffed, pretending I wasn't bothered. "I'll be OK. They're just a pack of dumb old wolves. I don't care."

"Of course you don't," Gavner smiled.

"Come," Mr Crepsley said, heading upstream. "We cannot stand here all night, pining over a few mangy wolves." I glared at him and he coughed uncomfortably. "You know," he added softly, "wolves never forget a face. The cub will remember you even when it is old and grey."

"Really?" I asked.

"Yes," he said, then turned and resumed walking. Gavner and Harkat fell in behind him. I glanced over my shoulder one last time at the departing wolves, sighed resignedly, then I picked up my bag and followed.

CHAPTER ELEVEN

WE CROSSED above the opening where the stream came tumbling out of the mountain. The noise was deafening, especially for super-sensitive vampire ears, so we hurried on as quickly as possible. The rocks were slippery and in some spots we had to form a chain. At one extra-icy patch, Gavner and me both slipped. I was in front, holding on to Mr Crepsley, but the force of the fall broke our grip. Luckily, Harkat held on to Gavner and pulled the two of us up.

We reached the mouth of a tunnel a quarter of an hour later. We hadn't climbed very far up the mountain, but it was a steep drop when I looked down. I was glad we weren't climbing any higher.

Mr Crepsley entered first. I went in after him. It was dark inside the tunnel. I was going to ask Mr Crepsley if we should stop to set torches, when I realized that the further in we crept, the brighter the tunnel became.

"Where's the light coming from?" I asked.

"Luminous lichen," Mr Crepsley replied.

"Is that a tongue-twister or an answer?" I grumbled.

"It's a form of fungus which gives off light," Gavner explained. "It grows in certain caves and on the floors of some oceans."

"Oh, right. Does it grow all over the mountain?"

"Not everywhere. We use torches where it doesn't." Ahead of us, Mr Crepsley stopped and cursed. "What's wrong?" Gavner asked.

"Cave-in," he sighed. "There is no way through."

"Does that mean we can't get in?" I asked, alarmed at the thought of having trekked all this way for nothing, only to have to turn back at the very end.

"There are other ways," Gavner said. "The mountain's riddled with tunnels. We'll just have to backtrack and find another."

"We had better hurry," Mr Crepsley said. "Dawn is fast approaching."

We shuffled back the way we'd come, Harkat in the lead this time. Outside, we moved as quickly as we could – which wasn't very fast, given the treacherous footing – and made it to the mouth of the next tunnel a few minutes after the sun had started to rise. This new tunnel wasn't as large as the other and the two full-vampires had to walk bent double. Harkat and me just had to duck our heads. The luminous lichen didn't grow strongly here, though there was enough of it for our extra-sharp eyes to see by.

After a while I noticed that we were sloping downwards instead of up. I asked Gavner about this. "It's just the way the tunnel goes," he said. "It'll lead upwards eventually."

About half an hour later, we cut up. At one stage the tunnel veered upwards almost vertically and we faced a difficult climb. The walls pressed tightly about us and I'm sure I wasn't the only one whose mouth dried up with nerves. Shortly after the tunnel levelled out, it opened on to a small cave, where we stopped to rest. I could hear the stream we'd crossed earlier churning along not far beneath our feet.

There were four tunnels leading out of the cave. I asked Gavner how Mr Crepsley knew which to take. "The correct tunnel's marked," he said, leading me over to them and pointing to a tiny arrow which had been scratched into the wall at the bottom of one tunnel.

"Where do the others lead?" I asked.

"Dead ends, other tunnels, or up to the Halls." The Halls were what they called the parts of the mountain where the vampires lived. "Many of the tunnels haven't been explored and there are no maps. Never wander off by yourself," he warned. "You could get lost very easily."

While the others were resting, I checked on Madam Octa, to see if she was hungry. She'd slept through most of the journey – she didn't like the cold – but woke every now and then to eat. As I was taking the cloth off her cage, I saw a spider creeping towards us. It wasn't as large as Madam Octa, but it looked dangerous.

"Gavner!" I called, stepping away from the cage.

"What's wrong?"

"A spider."

"Oh," he grinned. "Don't worry — the mountain's full of them."

"Are they poisonous?" I asked, bending down to study the spider, which was examining the cage with great interest.

"No," he answered. "Their bite's no worse than a bee sting."

I removed the cloth, curious to see what Madam Octa would do when she spotted the strange spider. She took no notice of it, just sat where she was, while the other spider crawled over the cage. I knew a lot about spiders — I'd read many books about arachnids and watched wildlife programmes when I was younger — but hadn't seen any quite like this one before. It was hairier than most, and a curious yellow colour.

Once the spider had departed, I fed Madam Octa a few insects and replaced the cloth. I lay down with the others and napped for a few hours. At one stage I thought I heard children giggling in one of the tunnels. I sat up, ears strained, but the sound didn't come to me again.

"What's wrong?" Gavner groaned softly, half-opening an eye.

"Nothing," I said uncertainly, then asked Gavner if any vampire children lived in the mountain.

"No," he said, closing his eye. "You're the only blooded kid, as far as I know."

"Then I must have been imagining things," I yawned, and lay down again, though I kept one ear cocked while I dozed.

*　*　*

Later we rose and proceeded further up the mountain, taking the tunnels marked with arrows. After what seemed an age we came to a large wooden door blocking the tunnel. Mr Crepsley made himself presentable, then knocked loudly with his bare knuckles. There was no immediate answer, so he knocked again, then again.

Finally there were sounds of life on the far side of the door and it opened. Torchlight flared from within. It was blinding to us after so long in the tunnels and we shielded our eyes until they'd adjusted.

A lean vampire in dark green clothes emerged and cast an eye over us. He frowned when he saw Harkat and me, and took a firmer grip on the long spear he was holding. I could see others behind him, dressed in green as well, none lacking a weapon.

"Address yourselves to the gate," the guard barked. The vampires had told me this was how newcomers were greeted.

"I am Larten Crepsley, come to seek Council," Mr Crepsley said. It was the standard reply.

"I am Gavner Purl, come to seek Council," Gavner said.

"I am Darren Shan, come to seek Council," I told the guard.

"I ... Harkat Mulds. Come ... seek Council," Harkat wheezed.

"Larten Crepsley is recognized by the gate," the guard said. "And Gavner Purl is recognized. But these other two..." He pointed his spear at us and shook his head.

"They are our travelling companions," Mr Crepsley said. "The boy is my assistant, a half-vampire."

"Do you vouch for him?" the guard asked.

"I do."

"Then Darren Shan is recognized by the gate." The tip of his spear pointed firmly at Harkat now. "But *this* is no vampire. What business has he at Council?"

"His name is Harkat Mulds. He is a Little Person. He—"

"A Little Person!" the guard gasped, lowering his spear. He crouched and made a rude study of Harkat's face (Harkat had removed his hood soon after we entered the tunnels, the better to see by). "He's an ugly specimen, isn't he?" the guard remarked. If he hadn't been carrying a spear, I'd have ticked him off for speaking so inconsiderately. "I thought the Little People couldn't speak."

"We all thought that," Mr Crepsley said. "But they can. At least, this one can. He has a message for the Princes, to be delivered in person."

"A message?" The guard scratched his chin with the tip of the spear. "From who?"

"Desmond Tiny," Mr Crepsley replied.

The guard blanched, stood to attention and said quickly, "The Little Person known as Harkat Mulds is recognized by the gate. The Halls are open to all of you. Enter and fare well."

He stepped aside and let us pass. Moments later the door closed behind us and our journey to the Halls of Vampire Mountain was at an end.

CHAPTER TWELVE

ONE OF the green-clad guards escorted us to the Hall of Osca Velm, which was a Hall of welcome (most of the Halls were named after famous vampires). This was a small cavern, the walls knobbly and black with the grime and soot of decades. It was warmed and lit by several open fires, the air pleasantly thick with smoke (the smoke slowly exited the cavern through natural cracks and holes in the ceiling). There were several roughly-carved tables and benches where arriving vampires could rest and eat (the legs of the tables had been fashioned from the bones of large animals). There were hand-woven baskets full of shoes on the walls, which newcomers were free to pick from. You could also find out who was in attendance at the Council — a large black stone was set in one of the walls, and the name of every vampire who'd arrived was etched upon it. As we sat at a long wooden table, I saw a vampire climb a ladder and add our names to the list. After Harkat's, he put in brackets, 'A Little Person'.

There weren't many vampires in the quiet, smoky Hall — ourselves, a few more who'd recently arrived, and several green-uniformed guards. A vampire with long hair, wearing no top, came over to us with two round barrels. One was packed to the top with loaves of hard bread, the other was half-full of gristly bits of both raw and cooked meat.

We took as much as we wished to eat and set it down on the table (there were no plates), using our fingers and teeth to break off chunks. The vampire returned with three large jugs, filled with human blood, wine and water. I asked for a mug, but Gavner told me you had to pour straight from the jug. It was difficult — I soaked my chin and chest with water the first time I tried — but it was more fun than drinking out of a cup.

The bread was stale, but the vampire brought bowls of hot broth (the bowls were carved from the skulls of various beasts), and the bread was fine if you tore a piece off and dipped it in the thick, dark broth for a few seconds. "This is great," I said, munching away at my third slice.

"The best," Gavner agreed. He was already on his fifth.

"How come you're not having any broth?" I asked Mr Crepsley, who was eating his bread plain.

"Bat broth does not agree with me," he replied.

My hand froze on its way to my mouth. The soaked piece of bread I'd been holding fell to the table. "*Bat* broth?" I yelped.

"Of course," Gavner said. "What did you think it was made of?"

I stared down into the dark liquid of the bowl. The light was poor in the cavern, but now that I focused, I spotted a thin, leathery wing sticking out of the broth. "I think I'm going to be sick!" I moaned.

"Don't be stupid," Gavner chortled. "You loved it when you didn't know what it was. Just get it down you and pretend it's nice fresh chicken soup — you'll eat a lot worse than bat broth before your stay in Vampire Mountain's over!"

I pushed the bowl away. "Actually, I feel quite full," I muttered. "I'll leave it for now." I glanced at Harkat, who was mopping up the last of his broth with a thick slice of bread. "You don't mind eating bats?" I asked.

Harkat shrugged. "I've no taste ... buds. Food is ... all the same ... to me."

"You can't taste *anything*?" I asked.

"Bat ... dog ... mud — no difference. I have no ... sense of smell ... either. That's why ... no nose."

"That's something I meant to ask about," Gavner said. "If you're not able to smell without a nose, how can you hear without ears?"

"I have ... ears," Harkat said. "They're under ... skin." He pointed to two spots on either side of his round green eyes. (He'd left his hood down.)

Gavner leant over the table to examine Harkat's ears. "I see them!" he exclaimed and we all leaned over to gawk. Harkat didn't mind — he liked the attention. His 'ears' looked like dry dates, barely visible beneath the grey skin.

"You can hear in spite of the skin stretched over them?" Gavner asked.

"Quite well," Harkat replied. "Not as ... good as vampires. But better ... than humans."

"How come you've got ears but no nose?" I asked.

"Mr Tiny ... didn't give me ... nose. Never asked ... why not. Maybe because ... of air. Would need ... another mask ... for nose."

It was strange to think that Harkat couldn't smell the musky air of the Hall or taste the bat broth. No wonder the Little People never complained when I brought them rotting, stinking animals that had been dead for ages!

I was about to ask Harkat more about his limited senses when an ancient-looking vampire dressed in red sat down opposite Mr Crepsley and smiled. "I was expecting you weeks ago," he said. "What took you so long?"

"Seba!" Mr Crepsley roared, and lunged across the table to clasp the older vampire's shoulders. I was surprised — I'd never seen him behave so warmly towards another person. He was beaming when he let the vampire go. "It has been a long time, old friend."

"Too long," the older vampire agreed. "I have often searched for you mentally, in the hope that you were near. When I sensed you coming, I hardly dared believe it."

The older vampire ran an eye over Harkat and me. He was wrinkled and shrunken with age, but the light of a younger man burned brightly in his eyes. "Are you going to introduce me to your friends, Larten?" he asked.

"Of course," Mr Crepsley said. "You know Gavner Purl."

"Gavner," the vampire nodded.

"Seba," Gavner replied.

"This is Harkat Mulds," Mr Crepsley said.

"A Little Person," Seba noted. "I have not seen one of those since Mr Tiny visited us when I was a boy. Greetings, Harkat Mulds."

"Hello," Harkat replied.

Seba blinked slowly. "He *talks*?"

"Wait until you hear what he has to say!" Mr Crepsley said sombrely. Then, turning to me, he said, "And this is Darren Shan — my assistant."

"Greetings, Darren Shan," Seba smiled at me. He looked at Mr Crepsley strangely. "You, Larten — with an assistant?"

"I know," Mr Crepsley coughed. "I always said I would never take one."

"And so young," Seba murmured. "The Princes will not approve."

"Most probably not," Mr Crepsley agreed miserably. Then he shook off his gloom. "Darren, Harkat — this is Seba Nile, the quartermaster of Vampire Mountain. Do not let his age fool you — he is as sly, cunning and quick as any vampire, and will get the better of those who try and best him."

"As you know from experience," Seba chuckled. "Do you remember when you set out to steal half a vat of my finest wine and replace it with a lesser vintage?"

"Please," Mr Crepsley said, looking pained. "I was young

and foolish. There is no need to remind me."

"What happened?" I asked, delighted by the vampire's discomfort.

"Tell him, Larten," Seba said, and Mr Crepsley obeyed sullenly, like a child.

"He got to the wine first," he muttered. "Emptied the vat and replaced the wine with vinegar. I had swallowed half a bottle before I realized. I spent the rest of the night retching."

"No!" Gavner burst out laughing.

"I was young," Mr Crepsley growled. "I did not know better."

"But I taught you, Larten, did I not?" Seba remarked.

"Yes," Mr Crepsley smiled. "Seba was my tutor. I learned most of what I know at his hands."

The three vampires got to talking about old times and I sat listening. Most of what they said sailed clean over my head – names of people and places which meant nothing to me – and after a while I sat back and gazed around the cavern, studying the flickering lights of the fires and the shapes the smoke made in the air. I only realized I was dozing off when Mr Crepsley shook me gently and my eyes snapped open.

"The boy is tired," Seba noted.

"He has never made the journey before," Mr Crepsley said. "He is not accustomed to such hardship."

"Come," Seba said, standing. "I will find rooms for you. He is not the only one who needs to rest. We will talk more tomorrow."

As the quartermaster of Vampire Mountain, Seba was in charge of the stores and living quarters. It was his job to make sure there was enough food and drink and blood for everyone, and that every vampire had a place to sleep. There were other vampires working for him, but he was the main man. Aside from the Princes, Seba was the most respected vampire in the mountain.

Seba bid me walk beside him as we made our way from the Hall of Osca Velm to our sleeping quarters. He pointed out various Halls as we passed, and told me their names — most of which I couldn't pronounce, never mind remember — and what they were used for.

"It will take a while to adjust," he said, noting my dazed gaze. "For the first few nights you may feel lost. But in time you will grow accustomed to the place."

The network of tunnels connecting the Halls to the sleeping quarters were cold and damp, despite the torches, but the tiny rooms — niches carved out of the rocks — were bright and warm, each lit by a powerful torch. Seba asked if we wanted one big room between us, or if we'd prefer separate quarters.

"Separate," Mr Crepsley immediately replied. "I had enough of Gavner's snoring on the trail."

"Charming!" Gavner huffed.

"Harkat and me don't mind doubling up, do we?" I said, not liking the idea of being left on my own in such a strange place.

"That's fine ... by me," Harkat agreed.

All the rooms boasted coffins instead of beds, but when Seba saw my gloomy face, he laughed and said I could have a hammock if I preferred. "I will send one of my staff to you tomorrow," he promised. "Tell him what you need and he will get it — I look after my guests!"

"Thank you," I said, glad that I wouldn't have to sleep in the coffin every day.

Seba started to leave. "Wait," Mr Crepsley called him back. "I have something to show you."

"Oh?" Seba smiled.

"Darren," Mr Crepsley said, "fetch Madam Octa."

When Seba Nile saw the spider, his breath caught in his throat and he gazed at it as though mesmerized. "Oh, Larten," he sighed, "what a beauty!" He took the cage from me – holding it tenderly – and opened the door.

"Stop!" I hissed. "Don't let her out — she's poisonous!"

Seba only smiled and reached into the cage. "I have never met a spider I have not been able to charm," he said.

"But–" I began.

"It is all right, Darren," Mr Crepsley said. "Seba knows what he is doing."

The old vampire coaxed the spider on to his fingers and lifted her out of the cage. She squatted comfortably in the palm of his hand. Seba bent his face over her and whistled softly. The spider's legs twitched, and from her intent look, I knew he must be communicating mentally with her.

Seba stopped whistling and Madam Octa crawled up his arm. Upon reaching his shoulder, she nestled up to his chin and relaxed. I couldn't believe it! I'd always had to whistle continuously – with a flute, not my lips – and concentrate fiercely to keep her from biting me, but with Seba she was completely docile.

"She is marvellous," Seba said, stroking her. "You must tell me more about her when you have a chance. I thought I knew of all the spiders in existence, but this one is new to me."

"I thought you would like her," Mr Crepsley beamed. "That is why I brought her. I wish to make you a present of her."

"You would part with such a wonderful spider?" Seba asked.

"For you, old friend — anything."

Seba smiled at Mr Crepsley, then looked at Madam Octa. Sighing regretfully, he shook his head. "I must refuse," he said. "I am old, and not as sprightly as I used to be. I am kept busy trying to keep up with jobs I once zipped through. I do not have the time to care for such an exotic pet."

"Are you sure?" Mr Crepsley asked, disappointed.

"I would love to take her but I cannot." He placed Madam Octa back in her cage and handed it to me. "Only the young have the energy to tend to the needs of spiders of such calibre. Look after her, Darren — she is beautiful and rare."

"I'll keep my eye on her," I promised. I once thought the spider was beautiful too, until she bit my best friend and led to me becoming a half-vampire.

"Now," Seba said, "I must go. You are not the only new arrives. Until we meet again — fare well."

There were no doors on the tiny rooms. Mr Crepsley and Gavner bid us goodnight, before heading for their coffins. Harkat and me stepped into our room and studied our two caskets.

"I don't think you'll fit in that," I said.

"That is ... OK. I can sleep ... on floor."

"In that case, see you in the morning." I glanced around the cave. "Or will it be night? Impossible to tell in here."

I didn't like getting into the coffin but took comfort in the fact that it was for one time only. Lying back, I left the lid open and stared up at the rocky grey ceiling. I thought that with the excitement of having arrived at Vampire Mountain, it'd take ages to fall asleep, but within minutes I'd dropped off and slept as soundly as I would have in my hammock back at the Cirque Du Freak.

CHAPTER THIRTEEN

HARKAT WAS standing by his coffin when I awoke, his green eyes wide open. I stretched and said good morning. There was a brief pause, then he shook his head and looked at me. "Good morning," he replied.

"Been awake long?" I asked.

"Just woke ... now. When you ... spoke to me. Fell asleep ... standing up."

I frowned. "But your eyes were open."

He nodded. "Always open. No lids ... or lashes. Can't shut them."

The more I learned about Harkat, the stranger he got! "Does that mean you can see things while you're asleep?"

"Yes, but I ... take no ... notice of them."

Gavner appeared at the entrance to our room. "Rise and shine, boys," he boomed. "Night's wearing on. There's work to be done. Anybody for bat broth?"

I asked to use the toilet before we went to eat. Gavner led me to a small door with the letters WC carved into it. "What does that stand for?" I asked.

"Water Closet," he informed me, then added, "Don't fall in!"

I thought that was a joke, but when I stepped inside, I realized it was a genuine warning — there was no toilet in the water closet, just a round hole in the ground which led to a gurgling mountain stream. I stared down the hole – it wasn't large enough for an adult to fall through, but somebody my size might just fit – and shivered when I saw dark, gushing water at the bottom. I didn't like the idea of squatting over the hole, but there was no other option, so I got on with it.

"Are all the toilets like that?" I asked when I came out.

"Yes," Gavner laughed. "It's the easiest way to get rid of the waste. There are several big streams leading out of the mountain and the toilets are built over them. The streams wash everything away."

Gavner led Harkat and me to the Hall of Khledon Lurt. Seba Nile had pointed out the Hall to me the day before and said it was where meals were served. He also told me a bit about Khledon Lurt; he had been a General of great standing, who'd died saving other vampires in the fight with the vampaneze, when they broke away.

Vampires loved telling tales of their ancestors. They kept few written records, opting instead to keep their history alive by word of mouth, passing on stories and legends around fires or over tables, one generation to another.

Red drapes hung from the ceiling, covering the walls, and there was a large statue of Khledon Lurt at the centre of the Hall. (Like most of the mountain's sculptures, it had been carved from the bones of animals.) The Hall was lit by strong torches, and it was nearly full when we arrived. Gavner, Harkat and me sat at a table with Mr Crepsley, Seba Nile and a load of vampires I didn't know. Talk was loud and raucous. Much of it had to do with fighting and feats of endurance.

This was my first good look at a crowd of vampires and I spent more time gazing around than I did eating. They didn't look that different to humans, except many were scarred from battle and hard living, and not a single one – it goes without saying! – was sun-tanned.

They were a smelly lot. They didn't use deodorants, though a few had strings of wild flowers or naturally scented herbs around their necks and wrists. Though vampires took care to wash in the world of humans – a foul stench could lead a vampire hunter to his prey – here in the mountain hardly any of them bothered with such luxuries. With all the soot and dirt of the Halls, they didn't see the point — it was impossible to keep clean.

I noticed virtually no women. After lengthy scanning, I spotted one sitting at a table in a corner, and another serving food. Otherwise, the vampires were all men. There were very few old people either; Seba seemed to be the oldest vampire present. I asked him about this.

"Very few vampires live to be a ripe old age," he replied.

"While vampires live far longer than humans, very few of us make it to our vampiric sixties or seventies."

"What do you mean?" I asked.

"Vampires measure age in two ways — earth years and vampire years," he explained. "The vampiric age is the age of the body — physically, I am in my eighties. The earth age refers to how many years a vampire has been alive — I was a young boy when I was blooded, so I am seven hundred earth years old."

Seven *hundred*! It was an incredible age.

"Though many vampires live for hundreds of earth years," Seba went on, "hardly any make it to their vampiric sixties."

"Why not?" I asked.

"Vampires live hard. We push ourselves to the limit, undergoing many tests of strength, wit and courage. Hardly any sit around in pyjamas and slippers, growing old quietly. Most, when they grow too old to care for themselves, meet death on their feet, rather than let their friends look after them."

"How come you've lived so long then?" I asked.

"Darren!" Mr Crepsley snapped, shooting me a piercing glare.

"Do not chastise the boy," Seba smiled. "His open curiosity is refreshing. I have lived to this long age because of my position," he said to me. "I was asked many decades ago to become the quartermaster of Vampire Mountain. It is not an enviable job, since it means living inside – hardly ever going hunting or fighting. But quartermasters are essential and much honoured — it would have been impolite of me to refuse. If I was free, I would have been long dead by now, but one who does not exert oneself tends to live longer than those who do."

"It seems crazy to me," I said. "Why do you push yourselves so hard?"

"It is our way," Seba answered. "Also, we have more time on our hands than humans, so it is less precious to us. If, in vampire years, a sixty-year-old man was blooded when he was twenty, he will have lived for more than four hundred earth years. A man grows tired of life when he has lived so much of it."

I was trying to see it from their point of view, but it was hard. Maybe I'd think differently when I'd been around a century or two!

Gavner rose before we'd finished eating and said he had to leave. He asked Harkat to accompany him.

"Where are you going?" I asked.

"The Hall of Princes," he said. "I must present myself to the Princes and tell them about the dead vampire and vampaneze we discovered. I also want to introduce Harkat, so he can pass on his message. The sooner the better, I think."

When they left, I asked Mr Crepsley why we hadn't gone with them. "It is not our place to present ourselves to the Princes," he said. "Gavner is a General, so he has the right to ask to see the Princes. As ordinary vampires, we must wait to be invited before them."

"But you used to be a General," I reminded him. "They wouldn't mind if you popped in to say hello, would they?"

"Of course they would," Mr Crepsley scowled, then turned to Seba and sighed. "He is slow to learn our ways."

Seba laughed. "And *you* are slow to learn the ways of the teacher. You forget how eagerly you questioned our way of life when you were blooded. I recall the night you stormed into my chambers and swore you would never become a General. You said Generals were backward imbeciles, and we should be looking to the future, not dwelling in the past."

"I never said that!" Mr Crepsley gasped.

"You certainly did," Seba insisted. "And more! You were a fiery youth, and there were times when I thought you would never calm down. I was often tempted to dismiss you, but I did not. I let you ask your questions and air your rage, and in time you learned that yours was not the wisest head in the world, and that the old ways might indeed be best.

"Students never appreciate their teachers while they are learning. It is only later, when they know more of the world, that they understand how indebted they are to those who instructed them. Good teachers expect no praise or love from the young. They wait for it, and in time, it comes."

"Are you scolding me?" Mr Crepsley asked.

"Yes," Seba smiled. "You are a fine vampire, Larten, but you have much to learn about teaching. Do not be so quick to criticize. Accept Darren's questions and stubbornness. Answer patiently and do not scold him for his opinions. Only in this way can he mature and develop as you did."

I extracted a guilty pleasure out of watching Mr Crepsley being hauled down a peg or two. I was extremely close to the vampire, but his pomposity sometimes got on my nerves. It was fun to see him have his wrists slapped!

"Stop smirking!" he snapped when he saw me.

"Now, now," I scolded him. "You heard what Mr Nile said — be *patient* — strive to *understand* me."

Mr Crepsley was puffing himself up to roar at me when Seba coughed discreetly. The vampire glanced at his old teacher, the air wheezed out of him, and he grinned sheepishly. Instead of giving out, he politely asked me to pass him a loaf of bread.

"My pleasure, Larten," I responded wryly, and the three of us shared a quiet laugh while the other vampires in the Hall of Khledon Lurt bellowed, told stories and cracked ribald jokes around us.

CHAPTER FOURTEEN

AFTER BREAKFAST, Mr Crepsley and me went to shower as we were filthy from the trek. He said we wouldn't wash often while here, but a shower at the start was a good idea. The Hall of Perta Vin-Grahl was a huge cavern with modest stalactites and two natural waterfalls, set close together to the right of the door. The water fell from high up into a vampire-made pond, and flowed to a hole near the back of the cavern, through which it disappeared and joined up with other streams underground.

"What do you think of the waterfalls?" Mr Crepsley asked, raising his voice to be heard over the noise of the running water.

"Beautiful," I said, admiring the way the torchlight reflected in the cascading water. "But where are the showers?"

Mr Crepsley grinned sadistically and I clicked to where we were meant to wash.

"No way!" I shouted. "The water must be freezing!"

"It is," Mr Crepsley agreed, slipping off his clothes, "but there are no other bathing facilities in Vampire Mountain."

I started to protest, but he laughed, walked to the nearest waterfall and immersed himself in the spray. I felt chilly just looking at the vampire showering, but I'd been eager to wash, and I knew he'd mock me for the rest of our stay if I backed out. So, wriggling free of my clothes, I walked to the edge of the pond, tested the water with my toes – *yowch!* – then leapt forward and surrendered myself to the flow of the second waterfall.

"Oh my lord!" I roared with ice-cold shock. "This is torture!"

"Aye!" Mr Crepsley shouted. "Now you understand why so few vampires bother to wash while at Council!"

"Is there a law against hot water?" I screeched, furiously scrubbing my chest, back and under my arms, in a hurry to finish with the shower.

"Not as such," Mr Crepsley replied, stepping out of his waterfall and running a hand through his short crop of orange hair, before shaking it dry like a dog. "But cold water is good enough for nature's other creatures of the wilds — we prefer not to heat it, at least not here, in the heart of our homeland."

Rough, prickly towels had been laid out close to the pond, and I wrapped myself in two of them as soon as I got out from under the waterfall. For a few minutes I felt as though my blood had turned to ice, but then my sensations returned and I was able to enjoy the warmth of the thick towels.

"Bracing," Mr Crepsley commented, rubbing himself dry.

"Murder, more like," I grumbled, though secretly I'd rather enjoyed the originality of the primitive shower.

While we were dressing, I stared at the rocky ceiling and walls and wondered how old the Halls were. I asked Mr Crepsley.

"Nobody knows exactly when vampires first came here or how they found it," he said. "The oldest discovered artefacts date back about three thousand years, but it is likely that for a long time it was only used occasionally, by small bands of wandering vampires.

"As far as we know, the Halls were established as a permanent base about fourteen hundred years ago. That is when the first Princes moved in and the Councils began. The Halls have grown since then. There are vampires at work on the structure all the time, hollowing out new rooms, extending old ones, building tunnels. It is long, tiring work — no mechanical equipment is allowed — but we have plenty of time to attend to it."

By the time we emerged from the Hall of Perta Vin-Grahl, word of Harkat's message had spread. He had told the Princes that the night of the Vampaneze Lord was at hand, and the vampires were in an uproar. They milled around the mountain like ants, passing on the word to those who hadn't heard, discussing it hotly and making absurd plans to set out and kill all the vampaneze they could find.

Mr Crepsley had promised to take me on a tour of the

Halls, but postponed it because of the commotion. He said we'd go when things quietened down — I might be trampled underfoot by agitated vampires if we set off now. I was disappointed, but knew he was right. This was no time to go exploring.

When we got back to my sleeping niche, a young vampire had taken away our coffins and was stringing up hammocks. He offered to find new clothes for Mr Crepsley and me if we wanted. We thanked him and accompanied him to one of the store-rooms to be kitted out. The stores of Vampire Mountain were full of treasures — food and blood vats and weapon caches — but I only got a brief look at these: the young vampire took us directly to the rooms where spare clothes were stored, and left us alone to pick whatever we liked.

I searched for a costume like my old one, but there were no pirate suits, so I chose a brown jumper and dark trousers, with a pair of soft shoes. Mr Crepsley dressed all in red — his favourite colour — though these robes were less fanciful than the ones he normally wore.

It was while he was adjusting his cape that I realized how similar his dress sense and Seba Nile's were. I mentioned it to him and he smiled. "I have copied many of Seba's ways," he said. "Not just his way of dressing, but also his way of speaking. I did not always use these precise, measured tones. When I was your age, I ran my words together the same as anybody. Years spent in the company of Seba taught me to slow down and consider my words before speaking."

"You mean I might end up like you one day?" I asked, alarmed at the thought of sounding so serious and stuffy.

"You might," Mr Crepsley said, "though I would not bet on it. Seba commanded my utmost respect, so I tried hard to copy what he did. You, on the other hand, seem to be determined to do the opposite of everything I say."

"I'm not *that* bad," I grinned, but there was some grain of truth in his words. I'd always been stubborn. I admired Mr Crepsley more than he knew, but hated the idea of looking like a pushover who did everything he was told. Sometimes I disobeyed the vampire just so he wouldn't think I was paying attention to what he said!

"Besides," Mr Crepsley added, "I have neither the heart nor the will to punish you when you make mistakes, as Seba punished me."

"Why?" I asked. "What did he do?"

"He was a fair but hard teacher," Mr Crepsley said. "When I told him of my desire to mimic him, he began paying close attention to my punctuation. Whenever I said 'don't' or 'it's' or 'can't' — he would pluck a hair from inside my nose!"

"No way!" I hooted.

"It is true," he said glumly.

"Did he use tweezers?"

"No — his fingernails."

"Ow!"

Mr Crepsley nodded. "I asked him to stop — I said I no longer cared to copy him — but he would not — he believes in finishing what one starts. After several months of having the hairs ripped from inside my nostrils, I had a brainwave, and singed them with a red-hot rod — not something I recommend you try! — so they would not grow back."

"What happened?"

Mr Crepsley blushed. "He began plucking hairs from an even more tender spot."

"Where?" I quickly asked.

The vampire's blush deepened. "I will not say — it is far too embarrassing."

(Later, when I got Seba by himself and put the question to him, he chortled wickedly and told me: "His *ears!*")

While we were slipping on our shoes, a slender, blond vampire in a bright blue suit barged into the room and slammed the door behind him. He stood panting by the door, unaware of us, until Mr Crepsley called to him. "Is that you, Kurda?"

"No!" the vampire yelled and grabbed for the handle. Then he paused and glanced over his shoulder. "Larten?"

"Yes," Mr Crepsley replied.

"That's different." The vampire sauntered over. When he got closer, I saw that he had three small red scars on his left cheek. They looked somehow familiar, though I couldn't think why. "I was hoping to run into you. I wanted to ask about this Harkat Mulds person and his message. Is it true?"

Mr Crepsley shrugged. "I have only heard the rumour. He said nothing to us about it on our way here." Mr Crepsley hadn't forgotten our promise to Harkat.

"Not a word of it?" the vampire asked, sitting on an upturned barrel.

"He told us the message was for the Vampire Princes only," I said.

The vampire eyed me curiously. "You must be the Darren Shan I've been hearing about." He shook my hand. "I'm Kurda Smahlt."

"What were you running from?" Mr Crepsley asked.

"Questions," Kurda groaned. "As soon as word of the Little Person and his message circulated, everyone ran to me to ask if it was true."

"Why should they ask *you*?" Mr Crepsley enquired.

"Because I know more about the vampaneze than most. And because of my investiture — it's amazing how much more you're expected to know when you move up in the world."

"Gavner Purl told me about that. Congratulations," Mr Crepsley said rather stiffly.

"You don't approve," Kurda noted.

"I did not say that."

"You didn't have to. It's written all over your face. But I don't mind. You're not the only one who objects. I'm used to the controversy."

"Excuse me," I said, "but what's an 'investiture'?"

"That's what they call it when you move up in the organization," Kurda explained. He had a light way of speaking, and a smile was never far from his lips and eyes. He reminded me of Gavner and I took an immediate shine to him.

"Where are you moving to?" I asked.

"The top," he smiled. "I'm being made a Prince. There'll

be a big ceremony and a lot of to-do." He grimaced. "It'll be a dull affair, I'm afraid, but there's no way around it. Centuries of tradition, standards to uphold, etcetera."

"You should not speak dismissively of your investiture," Mr Crepsley growled. "It is a great honour."

"I know," Kurda sighed. "I just wish people wouldn't make such a big deal of it. It's not like I've done anything wondrous."

"How *do* you become a Vampire Prince?" I asked.

"Why?" Kurda replied, a twinkle in his eye. "Thinking of applying for the job?"

"No," I chuckled. "Just curious."

"There's no fixed way," he said. "To become a General, you study for a set number of years and pass regular tests. Princes, on the other hand, are elected sporadically and for different reasons.

"Usually a Prince is someone who's distinguished himself in many battles, earning the trust and admiration of his colleagues. One of the established Princes nominates him. If the other Princes agree, he's automatically elevated up the ranks. If one objects, the Generals vote and the majority decision decides his fate. If two or more Princes object, the motion's rejected.

"I squeezed in by the vote," he grinned. "Fifty-four per cent of the Generals think I'll make a fitting Prince. Which means that near enough one in two think I won't!"

"It was the tightest vote ever," Mr Crepsley said. "Kurda is only a hundred and twenty earth years old, making him one of the youngest Princes ever, and many Generals believe he is too young to command their respect. They will follow him once he is elected — there is no question of that — but they are not happy about it."

"Come now," Kurda clucked. "Don't cover up for me and leave the boy thinking it's my age they object to. Here, Darren." When I was standing beside him, he bent his right arm so that the biceps were bulging. "What do you think?"

"They're not very big," I answered truthfully.

Kurda howled gleefully. "May the gods of the vampires save us from honest children! But you're right — they're *not* big. Every other Prince has muscles the size of bowling balls. The Princes have always been the biggest, toughest, bravest vampires. I'm the first to be nominated because of *this*." He tapped his head. "My *brain*."

"You mean you're smarter than everybody else?"

"Way smarter," he said, then pulled a face. "Not really," he sighed. "I just use my brains more than most. I don't believe vampires should stick to the old ways as rigidly as they do. I think we should move forward and adapt to life in the twenty-first century. More than anything else, I believe we should strive to make peace with our estranged brothers — the vampaneze."

"Kurda is the first vampire since the signing of the peace treaty to consort with the vampaneze," Mr Crepsley said gruffly.

"Consort?" I asked uncertainly.

"I've been meeting with them," Kurda explained. "I've spent much of the last thirty or forty years tracking them down, talking, getting to know them. That's where I got my scars." He tapped the left side of his face. "I had to agree to let them mark me — it was a way of offering myself to them and placing myself at their mercy."

Now I knew why the scars looked familiar — I'd seen similar marks on a human that the mad vampaneze Murlough had targeted six years earlier! Vampaneze were traditionalists and marked their prey in advance of a kill, always the same three scratches on the left cheek.

"The vampaneze aren't as different to us as most vampires believe," Kurda continued. "Many would jump at the chance to return to the fold. Compromises will have to be made — both sides must back down on certain issues — but I'm sure we can come to terms and live together again, as one."

"That is why he is being invested," Mr Crepsley said. "A lot of the Generals — fifty-four per cent, in any case — think it is time we were reunited with the vampaneze. The vampaneze trust Kurda but are reluctant to commit to negotiations with other Generals. When Kurda is a Prince, he will have total control over the Generals, and the vampaneze know no General would disobey the order of a Prince. So if he sends a vampire along to discuss terms, the vampaneze will trust him and sit down to talk. Or so the reasoning goes."

"You don't agree with it, Larten?" Kurda asked.

Mr Crepsley looked troubled. "There is much about the vampaneze which I admire, and I have never been opposed to talks designed to bridge the gap between us. But I would not be so quick to give them a voice among the Princes."

"You think they might use me to force more of their beliefs on us than we force on them?" Kurda suggested.

"Something like that."

Kurda shook his head. "I'm looking to create a tribe of equals. I won't force any changes through that the other Princes and Generals don't agree with."

"If that is so, luck to you. But things are happening too fast for my liking. Were I a General, I would have campaigned as hard as I could against you."

"I hope I live long enough to prove your distrust of me ill-founded," Kurda sighed, then turned to me. "What do *you* think, Darren? Is it time for a change?"

I hesitated before answering. "I don't know enough about the vampires or vampaneze to offer an opinion," I said.

"Nonsense," Kurda huffed. "Everyone's entitled to an opinion. Go on, Darren, tell me what you think. I like to know what's on people's minds. The world would be a simpler and safer place if we all spoke our true thoughts."

"Well," I said slowly, "I'm not sure I like the idea of doing a deal with the vampaneze — I think it's wrong to kill humans when you drink from them — but if you could persuade them to stop killing, it might be a good thing."

"This boy has brains," Kurda said, winking at me. "What you said just about sums up my own arguments in a nutshell. The killing of humans *is* deplorable and it's one of the concessions the vampaneze will have to make before a deal can be forged. But unless we draw them into talks and earn their trust, they'll never stop. Wouldn't it be worth giving up a few of our ways if we could stop the bloody murder?"

"Absolutely," I agreed.

"Hurm!" Mr Crepsley grunted, and would be drawn no further on the subject.

"Anyway," Kurda said, "I can't stay hidden forever. Time to return and fend off more questions. You're sure there's nothing you can tell me about the Little Person and his message?"

"Afraid not," Mr Crepsley said curtly.

"Oh well. I suppose I'll find out when I report to the Hall of Princes and see him myself. I hope you enjoy your stay in Vampire Mountain, Darren. We must get together once the chaos has died down and have a proper chat."

"I'd like that," I said.

"Larten," he saluted Mr Crepsley.

"Kurda."

He let himself out.

"Kurda's nice," I remarked. "I like him."

Mr Crepsley glanced at me sideways, stroked the long scar on his own left cheek, gazed thoughtfully at the door Kurda had left by, and again went, "Hurm!"

CHAPTER FIFTEEN

A COUPLE of long, quiet nights passed. Harkat had been kept in the Hall of Princes to answer questions. Gavner had General business to attend to and we only saw him when he crawled back to his coffin to sleep. I hung out with Mr Crepsley in the Hall of Khledon Lurt most of the time – he had a lot of catching up to do with old friends he hadn't seen in many years – or down in the stores with him and Seba Nile.

The elderly vampire was more disturbed by Harkat's message than most. He was the second oldest vampire in the Mountain – the oldest was a Prince, Paris Skyle, who was more than eight hundred – and the only one who'd been here when Mr Tiny visited and made his announcement all those centuries ago.

"A lot of today's vampires do not believe the old myths," he said. "They think Mr Tiny's warning was something we made up to frighten young vampires. But I remember how he looked. I recall the way his words echoed around the Hall of Princes, and the fear they instilled in everyone. The Vampaneze Lord is no mere figure of legend. He is real. And now, it seems, he is coming."

Seba lapsed into silence. He'd been drinking a mug of warm ale but had lost interest in it.

"He has not come yet," Mr Crepsley said spiritedly. "Mr Tiny is as old as time itself. When he says the night is at hand, he might mean hundreds or thousands of years from now."

Seba shook his head. "We have had our hundreds of years — seven centuries to make a stand and tackle the vampaneze. We should have finished them off, regardless of the consequences. Better to have been driven to the point of extinction by humans than wiped out entirely by the vampaneze."

"That is foolish talk," Mr Crepsley snapped. "I would rather take my chances with a mythical Vampaneze Lord than a real, stake-wielding human. So would you."

Seba nodded glumly and sipped at his ale. "You are probably right. I am old. My brain does not work as sharply as it used to. Perhaps my worries are those of an old man who has lived too long. Still..."

Such pessimistic words were on everybody's lips. Even those who scoffed outright at the idea of a Vampaneze Lord always seemed to end with a 'still...' or 'however...' or 'but...' The tension was clogging the dusty mountain air of the tunnels and Halls, constantly building, stifling all present.

The only one who didn't seem troubled by the rumours was Kurda Smahlt. He turned up outside our chambers, as upbeat as ever, the third night after Harkat had delivered his message.

"Greetings," he said. "I've had a hectic two nights, but things are calming down at last and I've a few free hours. I thought I'd take Darren on a tour of the Halls."

"Great!" I beamed. "Mr Crepsley was going to take me but we never got round to it."

"You don't mind if I escort him, Larten?" Kurda asked.

"Not in the slightest," Mr Crepsley said. "I am overwhelmed that one of your eminence has found the time to act as a guide so close to your investiture." He said it cuttingly, but Kurda ignored the elder vampire's sarcasm.

"You can tag along if you want," Kurda offered cheerfully.

"No thank you," Mr Crepsley smiled thinly.

"OK," Kurda said. "Your loss. Ready, Darren?"

"Ready," I said, and off we set.

* * *

Kurda took me to see the kitchens first. They were huge caves, built deep beneath most of the Halls. Large fires burned brightly. The cooks worked in shifts around the clock during times of Council. They had to in order to feed all the visitors.

"It's quieter the rest of the time," Kurda said. "There are usually no more than thirty vampires in residence. You often have to cook for yourself if you don't eat with the rest at the set times."

From the kitchens we progressed to the breeding Halls, where sheep, goats and cows were kept and bred. "We'd never be able to ship in enough milk and meat to feed all the vampires," Kurda explained when I asked why live animals were kept in the mountain. "This isn't an hotel, where you can ring a supplier and re-stock any time you please. Shipping in food is an enormous hassle. It's easier to rear the animals ourselves and butcher them when we need to."

"What about human blood?" I asked. "Where does that come from?"

"Generous donors," Kurda winked, and led me on. (I only realized much later that he'd side-stepped the question.)

The Hall of Cremation was our next stop. It was where vampires who died in the mountain were cremated. "What if they don't want to be cremated?" I asked.

"Oddly enough, hardly any vampires ask to be buried," he mused. "Perhaps it has something to do with all the time they spend in coffins while they're alive. However, if someone requests a burial, their wishes are respected.

"Not so long ago, we'd lower the dead into an underground stream, and let the water wash them away. There's a cave, far below the Halls, where one of the larger streams opens up. It's called the Hall of Final Voyage, though it's never used now. I'll show it to you if we're ever down that way."

"Why should we be down there?" I asked. "I thought those tunnels were only used to get in and out of the mountain."

"One of my hobbies is map-making," Kurda said. "I've been trying to make accurate maps of the mountain for decades. The Halls are easy but the tunnels are much more difficult. They've never been mapped and a lot are in poor shape. I try to get down to them whenever I return, to map out a few more unknown regions, but I don't have as much time to work on them as I'd like. I'll have even less when I'm a Prince."

"It sounds like an interesting hobby," I said. "Could I come with you the next time you go mapping? I'd like to see how it's done."

"You're really interested?" He sounded surprised.

"Why shouldn't I be?"

He laughed. "I'm used to vampires falling asleep whenever I start talking about maps. Most have no interest in such mundane matters. There's a saying among vampires: 'Maps are for humans'. Most vampires would rather discover new territory for themselves, regardless of the dangers, than follow directions on a map."

The Hall of Cremation was a large octagonal room with a high ceiling full of cracks. There was a pit in the middle – where the dead vampires were burnt – and a couple of long, gnarly benches on the far side, made out of bones. Two women and a man were sitting on the benches, whispering to each other, and a young child was at their feet, playing with a scattering of animal bones. They didn't have the appearance of vampires – they were thin and ill-looking, with lank hair and rags for clothes; their skin was deathly pale and dry, and their eyes were an eerie white colour. The adults stood when we entered, grabbed the child and withdrew through a door at the back of the room.

"Who were they?" I asked.

"The Guardians of this chamber," Kurda replied.

"Are they vampires?" I pressed. "They didn't look like vampires. And I thought I was the only child vampire in the mountain."

"You are," Kurda said.

"Then who—"

"Ask me later!" Kurda snapped with unusual briskness. I blinked at his sharp tone, and he smiled an immediate apology. "I'll tell you about them when our tour is complete," he said softly. "It's bad luck to talk about them here. Though I'm not superstitious by nature, I prefer not to test the fates where the Guardians are concerned."

(Although he'd aroused my curiosity, I wasn't to learn more about the strange, so-called Guardians until much later, as by the end of our tour I was in no state to ask any questions, and had forgotten about them entirely.)

Letting the matter of the Guardians drop, I examined the cremation pit, which was just a hollow dip in the ground. There were leaves and sticks in the bottom, waiting to be lit. Large pots were set around the hole, a club-like stick in each. I asked what they were for.

"Those are pestles, for the bones," Kurda said.

"What bones?"

"The bones of the vampires. Fire doesn't burn bones.

Once a fire's burnt out, the bones are extracted, put in the pots, and ground down to dust with the pestles."

"What happens to the dust?" I asked.

"We use it to thicken bat broth," Kurda said earnestly, then burst out laughing as my face turned green. "I'm joking! The dust is thrown to the winds around Vampire Mountain, setting the spirit of the dead vampire free."

"I'm not sure I'd like that," I commented.

"It's better than burying a person and leaving them to the worms," Kurda said. "Although, personally speaking, I want to be stuffed and mounted when my time comes." He paused a moment, then burst out laughing again.

Leaving the Hall of Cremation, we set off for the three Halls of Sport (individually they were called the Hall of Basker Wrent, the Hall of Rush Flon'x, and the Hall of Oceen Pird, though most vampires referred to them simply as the Halls of Sport). I was eager to see the gaming Halls, but as we made our way there, Kurda paused in front of a small door, bowed his head, closed his eyes and touched his eyelids with his fingertips.

"Why did you do that?" I asked.

"It's the custom," he said, and moved on. I stayed, staring at the door.

"What's this Hall called?" I asked.

Kurda hesitated. "You don't want to go in there," he said.

"Why not?" I pressed.

"It's the Hall of Death," he said quietly.

"Another cremation Hall?"

He shook his head. "A place of execution."

"*Execution?*" I was really curious now. Kurda saw this and sighed.

"You want to go in?" he asked.

"Can I?"

"Yes, but it's not a pretty sight. It would be better to proceed directly to the Halls of Sport."

A warning like that only made me more eager to see what lurked behind the door! Noting this, Kurda opened it and led me in. The Hall was poorly lit, and at first I thought it was deserted. Then I spotted one of the white-skinned Guardians, sitting in the shadows of the wall at the rear. He didn't rise or give any sign that he saw us. I started to ask Kurda about him, but the General shook his head instantly and hissed quietly, "I'm definitely not talking about them *here!*"

I could see nothing awful about the Hall. There was a pit in the centre of the floor and light wooden cages set against the walls, but otherwise it was bare and unremarkable.

"What's so bad about this place?" I asked.

"I'll show you," Kurda said, and guided me towards the edge of the pit. Looking down into the gloom, I saw dozens of sharpened poles set in the floor, pointing menacingly towards the ceiling.

"Stakes!" I gasped.

"Yes," Kurda said softly. "This is where the legend of the stake through the heart originated. When a vampire's brought to the Hall of Death, he's placed in a cage – that's what the cages against the walls are for – which is attached to ropes and hoisted above the pit. He's then dropped from a height and impaled on the stakes. Death is often slow and painful, and it's not unusual for a vampire to have to be dropped three or four times before he dies."

"But *why?*" I was appalled. "Who do they kill here?"

"The old or crippled, along with mad and treacherous vampires," Kurda answered. "The old or crippled vampires ask to be killed. If they're strong enough, they prefer to fight to the death, or wander off into the wilderness to die hunting. But those who lack the strength or ability to die on their feet ask to come here, where they can meet death face-on and die bravely."

"That's horrible!" I cried. "The elderly shouldn't be killed off!"

"I agree," Kurda said. "I think the nobility of the vampires is misplaced. The old and infirm often have much to offer, and I personally hope to cling to life as long as possible. But most vampires hold to the ancient belief that they can only lead worthwhile lives as long as they're fit enough to fend for themselves.

"It's different with mad vampires," he went on. "Unlike the vampaneze, we choose not to let our insane members run loose in the world, free to torment and prey on humans. Since they're too difficult to imprison — a mad vampire will claw his way through a stone wall — execution is the most humane way to deal with them."

"You could put them in straitjackets," I suggested.

Kurda smiled sourly. "There hasn't been a straitjacket

invented that could hold a vampire. Believe me, Darren, killing a mad vampire is a mercy, to the world in general and the vampire himself.

"The same goes for treacherous vampires," he added, "though there have been precious few of those — loyalty is something we excel at; one of the bonuses of sticking to the old ways so rigidly. Aside from the vampaneze – when they broke away, they were called traitors; many were captured and killed – there have been only six traitors executed in the fourteen hundred years that vampires have lived here."

I stared down at the stakes and shivered, imagining myself tied in a cage, hanging above the pit, waiting to fall.

"Do you give them blindfolds?" I asked.

"The mad vampires, yes, because it is merciful. Vampires who have *chosen* to die in the Hall of Death prefer to do without one — they like to look death in the eye, to show they're not afraid. Traitors, meanwhile, are placed in the cages face upwards, so their backs are to the stakes. It's a great dishonour for a vampire to die from stab wounds in the back."

"I'd rather get it in the back than the front," I snorted.

Kurda smiled. "Hopefully, you'll never get it in either!" Then, clapping my shoulder, he said, "This is a gloomy place, best avoided. Let's go play some games." And he swiftly ushered me out of the Hall, eagerly leaving behind its mysterious Guardian, the cages and the stakes.

CHAPTER SIXTEEN

THE HALLS of Sport were gigantic caverns, full of shouting, cheering, high-spirited vampires. They were exactly what I needed to perk me up after the disturbing visit to the Halls of Cremation and Death.

Various contests took place in each of the three Halls. They were mostly games of physical combat — wrestling, boxing, karate, weightlifting and so on — though speed chess was also strongly favoured, since it sharpened one's reactions and wits.

Kurda found seats for us near a wrestling circle and we watched as vampires tried to pin their opponents down or toss them out of the ring. You needed a quick eye to keep up with the action — vampires moved far faster than humans. It was like watching a fight on video while keeping the fast-forward button pressed.

The bouts weren't just faster than their human equivalents

— they were more violent too. Broken bones, bloody faces and bruises were the order of the night. Sometimes, Kurda told me, the damage was even worse — vampires could be killed taking part in these games, or injured so badly that a trip to the Hall of Death was all they had to look forward to.

"Why don't they wear protective clothing?" I asked.

"They don't believe in it," Kurda said. "They'd rather have their skulls cracked than wear helmets." He sighed morosely. "There are times when I think I don't know my people at all. Maybe I'd have been better off if I'd remained human."

We moved to another ring. In this one, vampires jabbed at each other with spears. It was a bit like fencing – you had to prick or cut an opponent three times to win – only a lot more dangerous and bloody.

"It's horrendous," I gasped as a vampire had half his upper arm sliced open, only to laugh and compliment his foe for making a good strike.

"You should see it when they play for real," someone said behind us. "They're just warming up at the moment." Turning, I saw a ginger-haired vampire who had only one eye. He was clad in a dark blue leather tunic and trousers. "They call this game the eye-baller," he informed me, "because so many people lose an eye or two playing it."

"Is that how you lost yours?" I asked, staring at his empty left eye socket and the scars around it.

"No," he chuckled. "I lost mine in a tussle with a lion."

"Honest?" I gasped.

"Honest."

"Darren, this is Vanez Blane," Kurda introduced us. "Vanez, this is—"

"—Darren Shan," Vanez nodded, shaking my hand. "I know him from the gossip. It's been a long time since one his age trod the Halls of Vampire Mountain."

"Vanez is a games master," Kurda explained.

"You're in charge of the games?" I asked.

"Hardly in charge," Vanez said. "The games are beyond the control of even the Princes. Vampires fight — it's in our blood. If not here, where their injuries can be tended to, then in the open, where they might bleed to death unaided. I keep an eye on things, that's all." He grinned.

"He also trains vampires to fight," Kurda said. "Vanez is one of our most valued instructors. Most Generals of the last hundred years have studied under him. Myself included." He rubbed the back of his head and grimaced.

"Still sore about that time I knocked you unconscious with a mace, Kurda?" Vanez enquired politely.

"You wouldn't have had the chance if I'd known what it was in advance," Kurda sulked. "I thought it was a bowl of incense!"

Vanez bellowed with laughter and slapped his knees. "You always were a bright one, Kurda — except when it came to the tools of war. One of my worst pupils," he told me. "Fast as an eel, and wiry, but he hated getting his hands bloody. A shame, as he would have been a wonder with a spear if he'd set his mind to it."

"There's nothing wonderful about losing an eye in a fight," Kurda huffed.

"There is if you win," Vanez disagreed. "Any injury's acceptable as long as you emerge victorious."

We watched the vampires cutting each other to pieces for another half an hour – nobody lost an eye while we were there – then Vanez led us round the Halls, explaining the games to me and how they served to toughen vampires up and prepare them for life in the outside world.

All manner of weapons hung from the walls of the Halls – some antiques, some for general use – and Vanez told me their names and how they were used; he even got a few down to demonstrate. They were fearsome instruments of destruction —— jagged spears, sharp axes, long and glinting knives, heavy maces, blade-edged boomerangs which could kill from eighty metres, clubs with thick spikes sticking out of them, stone-head war hammers which could cave in a vampire's skull with one well-placed blow. After a while I noticed there were no guns or bows and arrows, and asked about their absence.

"Vampires only fight hand to hand," Vanez informed me. "We do not use missile devices, such as guns, bows or slings."

"Never?" I asked.

"Never!" he said firmly. "Our reliance on hand weapons is sacred to us – to the vampaneze as well. Any vampire who resorted to a gun or bow would be held in contempt for the rest of his life."

"Things used to be even more backwards," Kurda chipped in. "Until two hundred years ago, a vampire was only supposed to use a weapon of his own making. Every vampire had to fashion his own knives, spears and clubs. Now, thankfully, that's no longer the case, and we can use store-bought equipment; but many vampires still cling to the old ways, and most of the weapons used during Council are handmade."

Moving away from the weapons, we stopped beside a series of overlapping narrow planks. Vampires were balancing on the planks and crossing from one to another, trying to knock their opponents to the ground with long round-ended staffs. There were six vampires in action when we arrived. A few minutes later, only one remained aloft — a woman.

"Well done, Arra," Vanez clapped. "Your sense of balance is as awesome as ever."

The female vampire leapt from the plank and landed beside us. She was dressed in a white shirt and beige trousers. She had long dark hair, tied behind her back. She wasn't especially pretty – she had a hard, weathered face – but after so much time spent staring at ugly, scarred vampires, she looked like a movie star to me.

"Kurda, Vanez," she greeted the vampires, then fixed her cool grey eyes on me. "And you are Darren Shan." She sounded decidedly unimpressed.

"Darren, this is Arra Sails," Kurda said. I stuck out a hand but she ignored it.

"Arra doesn't shake the hands of those she doesn't respect," Vanez whispered.

"And she respects precious few of us," Kurda said aloud. "Still refusing to shake hands with *me*, Arra?"

"I will never shake the hand of one who does not fight," she grunted. "When you become a Prince, I will bow to you and do your bidding, but I will never shake your hand, even under threat of execution."

"I don't think Arra voted for me in the election," Kurda said humorously.

"*I* didn't vote for you either," Vanez said, with a wicked grin.

"See what an average day is like for me, Darren?" Kurda groaned. "Half the vampires here love to rub my nose in the fact that they didn't vote for me, while the half who *did* almost never admit it in public, for fear the others would look down their noses at them."

"Never mind," Vanez chuckled. "We'll all have to kow-tow to you when you're a Prince. We're just getting our digs in while we can."

"Is it illegal to make fun of a Prince?" I asked.

"Not as such," Vanez said. "It just isn't done."

I examined Arra while she was picking a splinter from one of the rounded ends of her staff. She seemed to be as tough as any male vampire, not as burly, but just as muscular. While studying her, I got to thinking about how few female vampires I'd seen, and asked about it.

There was a long silence. The two men looked embarrassed. I was going to let the matter drop when Arra glanced at me archly and said, "Women do not make good vampires. The entire clan's barren, so the life doesn't appeal to many of us."

"Barren?" I enquired.

"We can't have children," she said.

"What — *none* of you?"

"It's something to do with our blood," Kurda said. "No vampire can sire or bear a child. The only way we can add to our ranks is by blooding humans."

I was stunned. Of course, I should have long ago stopped to wonder why there were no vampire children, and why everyone was so surprised to meet a young half-vampire. But I'd so much else on my mind, I never really paused to consider it.

"Does that rule apply to half-vampires too?" I asked.

"I'm afraid so," Kurda said, frowning. "Larten never mentioned it?"

I shook my head numbly. I couldn't have children! It wasn't something I'd thought about much — seeing as how I aged at a fifth the human rate, it would be a long time before I was ready to become a parent — but I'd always assumed I'd have the choice. It was alarming to learn that I could never father a son or daughter.

"This is bad," Kurda muttered. "This is very, very bad."

"What do you mean?" I asked.

"Vampires are supposed to inform new recruits of such things before they blood them. It's one of the reasons we almost never blood children — we prefer new vampires to know what they're getting into and what they're giving up. To blood a boy your age was bad enough, but to do it without telling you all the facts..." Kurda shook his head glumly and shared an uncertain look with Arra and Vanez.

"You'll have to tell the Princes about this," Arra sniffed.

"They must be informed," Kurda agreed, "but I'm sure Larten means to tell them himself. I'll wait and let him speak. It would be unfair to jump in before he has a chance to put his side of the story forward. Will you two keep this to yourselves?"

Vanez nodded and, moments later, Arra did too. "But if he doesn't make mention of it soon..." Arra growled threateningly.

"I don't understand," I said. "Will Mr Crepsley get into trouble for blooding me?"

Kurda shared another glance with Arra and Vanez. "Probably not," he said, trying to make light of it. "Larten's a sly old vampire. He knows the ropes. I'm sure he'll be able to explain it away to the satisfaction of the Princes."

"Now," Vanez said before I could ask any more questions, "how would you like to try out the bars with Arra?"

"You mean have a go on the planks?" I asked, thrilled.

"I'm sure we can find a staff to suit you. How about it, Arra? Any objections to fighting a smaller opponent?"

"It will be a novel experience," the vampiress mused. "I'm accustomed to tackling men larger than myself. It will be interesting to fight one smaller."

She hopped up on to the planks and twirled her staff over her head and under her arms. It spun faster than my eyes could follow, and I began having second thoughts about getting up there with her; but I'd look like a coward if I backed out now.

Vanez found a staff small enough for me and spent a few minutes showing me how to use it. "Hold it in the middle," he instructed. "That way you can attack with either end. Don't swing too hard or you'll leave yourself open to a counterstrike. Jab at her legs and stomach. Forget about her head — you're too short to aim so high. Try tripping her. Go for her knees and toes — those are the soft points."

"What about defending himself?" Kurda interrupted. "I think that's more important. It's been eleven years since Arra was beaten on the bars. Show him how to stop her cracking his head open, Vanez, and forget the other stuff."

Vanez showed me how to block low jabs and sideswipes and overhead cuts. "The trick is keeping your balance," he said. "Fighting on the bars isn't like fighting on the ground. You can't just block a blow — you have to stay steady on your feet, so you're ready for the next. Sometimes it's better to take a strike than duck out of the way."

"Nonsense," Kurda snorted. "Duck all you like, Darren — I don't want to cart you back to Larten on a stretcher!"

"She won't really hurt me, will she?" I asked, alarmed.

Vanez laughed. "Of course not. Kurda's only winding you up. She won't go easy on you — Arra doesn't know how to take things easy — but I'm sure she won't set out to seriously harm you." He glanced up at Arra and muttered under his breath, "At least, I *hope* she won't!"

CHAPTER SEVENTEEN

I SLIPPED my shoes off and mounted the bars. I spent a minute or two getting used to them, shuffling around, focusing on my balance. It was easy without the staff — vampires have a great sense of balance — but awkward with it. I took a few practice swipes and almost fell off straightaway.

"Short jabs!" Vanez snapped, darting forward to steady me. "Broad swings will be the end of you."

I did as Vanez instructed and soon had the hang of it. A couple more minutes hopping from one bar to another, crouching and jumping, and I was ready.

We met in the middle of the bars and knocked our staffs together in salute. Arra was smiling — she obviously didn't think much of my chances. We nudged away from each other and Vanez clapped his hands to signal the start of the fight.

Arra attacked immediately and jabbed at my stomach with the end of her staff. As I pulled out of her way, she swept her

127

staff round in a vicious circle and brought it down on top of me — a skull-cracker! I managed to raise my staff in time to divert the blow, but the jolt of the contact ran through the staff and my fingers to the rest of my body, and forced me to my knees. My grasp on the staff slipped, but I caught it before it fell.

"Are you out to kill him?" Kurda shouted angrily.

"The bars are no place for little boys who can't protect themselves," Arra sneered.

"I'm calling an end to this," Kurda huffed, striding towards me.

"As you wish," Arra said, lowering her staff and turning her back on me.

"No!" I grunted, getting to my feet and raising my staff.

Kurda stopped short. "Darren, you don't have to—" he began.

"I want to," I interrupted. Then, to Arra, "Come on — I'm ready."

Arra smiled as she faced me, but now it was an admiring smile, not a mocking one. "The half-vampire has spirit. It's good to know that the young aren't entirely spineless. Now let's see what it takes to drive the spirit out of you."

She attacked again, short chopping swipes, switching from left to right without warning. I blocked the blows as best I could, though I had to take some on my arms and shoulders. I retreated to the end of the plank, slowly, guarding myself, then leapt out of her way as she took a wide swing at my legs.

Arra hadn't anticipated the jump and was thrown off-balance. I used the moment to launch my first blow of the contest and hit her firmly on her left thigh. It didn't seem to hurt her much, but she hadn't been expecting it and let out a roar of surprise.

"A point to Darren!" Kurda whooped.

"We don't score this on points," Arra snarled.

"You'd better watch yourself, Arra," Vanez chuckled, his single eye a-gleam. "I think the boy has the beating of you. You'll never be able to show your face in the Halls again if a teenage half-vampire bests you on the bars."

"The night I'm bested by the likes of him is the night you can strap me into a cage in the Hall of Death and drop me on the stakes," Arra growled. She was angry now – she didn't like being baited by those on the ground – and when next she faced me, her smile had disappeared.

I moved cautiously. I knew that one good strike meant nothing. If I grew cocky and dropped my guard, she'd finish me off in no time. As she stepped across to face me, I edged backwards. I let her advance a couple of metres, then leapt to another bar. After a few retreating steps, I jumped to another bar, then another.

I was hoping to frustrate Arra. If I could drag the contest out, she might lose her temper and do something silly. But a vampire's patience is legendary and Arra was no exception. She trailed me like a cat after a bird, ignoring the jeers of those who'd gathered round the bars to observe the fight, taking her time, letting me play my evasive games, waiting for the right moment to strike.

Eventually she manoeuvred me into a corner and I had to fight. I got in a couple of low blows – hitting her toes and knees as Vanez had suggested – but there was no power in my shots and she took them without blinking. As I stooped to hit her toes again, she leapt to an adjoining bar and brought the flat of her staff down over my back. I roared with pain and dropped on to my belly. My staff fell to the floor.

"Darren!" Kurda shouted, rushing forward.

"Leave him!" Vanez snapped, holding the General back.

"But he's hurt!"

"He'll live. Don't disgrace him in front of all these vampires. Let him fight."

Kurda didn't like it, but he did as Vanez said.

Arra, meanwhile, had decided I was finished. Rather than strike me with her staff, she eased one of the rounded ends under my belly and tried rolling me off the bar. She was smiling again. I let my body roll, but held on tight to the bar with my hands and feet, so I didn't fall off. I swung right the way around, until I was hanging on upside down, snatched my staff off the ground and jabbed it between Arra's calves. With a sharp twist, I sent her sprawling. She shrieked, and for a split second I was sure I'd knocked her off and won, but she grabbed for the bar on her way down and held on, as I was doing. Her staff, however, struck the floor and spun away.

The vampires who'd gathered to watch – there were twenty or thirty around the bars now – clapped loudly as we hauled ourselves back to our feet and eyed each other warily. I lifted my staff and smiled. "Seems like *I* have the advantage now," I noted cockily.

"Not for long," Arra grunted. "I'm going to rip that staff out of your hands and smash your head in with it!"

"Is that so?" I grinned. "Come on then — let's see you try!"

Arra spread her hands and closed in on me. I hadn't really expected her to attack without her staff and wasn't sure what to do. I didn't like the idea of striking an unarmed opponent, especially a woman.

"You can pick your staff up if you want," I offered.

"Leaving the bars isn't allowed," she replied.

"Get someone to bring it to you then."

"That's not allowed either."

I retreated. "I don't want to hit you when you've nothing to defend yourself with," I said. "How about I throw away my staff as well and we fight hand to hand?"

"A vampire who abandons his weapon is a fool," Arra said. "If you throw the staff away, I'll ram it down your throat to teach you a lesson when we're through up here on the bars."

"OK!" I snapped irritably. "Have it your own way." I stopped retreating, raised my staff and laid into her.

Arra was hunched over — she had a lower centre of gravity that way and would be harder to knock off — so I was able to aim at her head. I jabbed at her face with the end of my staff. She avoided the first couple of blows, but I struck her cheek with the third. It didn't draw blood, but left a nasty welt.

Arra was retreating now. She gave ground grudgingly, standing up to my lesser strikes, taking them on her arms and hands, only backing up to avoid the heavier blows. Despite my earlier warning to myself, I grew over-confident. I thought I had her where I wanted. Instead of taking my time and finishing her off slowly, I went for the quick kill, and that proved my undoing.

I flicked the end of my staff towards the side of her head, planning to sting her ear. It was a casual swipe, neither as sharp nor as fast as it needed to be. I connected with her ear, but there was no power in the shot. Before I could draw back for my next, Arra's hands sprang into action.

Her right hand grasped the end of my staff and held it tight. Her left hand balled up into a fist and smashed into my jaw. She hit me again and I saw stars. As she drew back her fist for a third punch, I reacted automatically and stepped clear of her reach, which was when she gave a quick wrench and ripped my staff away from me.

"Now!" she hooted triumphantly, twirling the staff over her head. "Now who has the advantage?"

"Take it easy, Arra," I said nervously, backing away from her like crazy. "I offered to give you your staff back, remember?"

"And I refused," she snorted.

"Let him have a staff, Arra," Kurda said. "You can't expect him to defend himself with his bare hands. It isn't fair."

"How about it, *boy*?" she asked. "I'll let you call for a replacement staff if you wish." By her tone, I knew she wouldn't think much of me if I did.

I shook my head. I'd have traded anything I owned for a

staff, but I wasn't about to ask for special favours, not when Arra hadn't. "That's OK," I said. "I'll fight on like I am."

"Darren!" Kurda howled. "Don't be stupid. Call it off if you don't want another staff. You've fought bravely and proved your courage."

"There would be no shame in quitting now," Vanez agreed.

I stared into Arra's eyes, saw that she expected me to resign, and stopped. "No," I said. "No quitting. I won't get off these bars till I'm knocked off." I started forward, hunched over like Arra had been.

Arra blinked, surprised, then raised her staff and set about ending the contest. It didn't take long. I blocked her first jab with my left hand, took her second in the belly, ducked out of the way of her third, slapped away her fourth with my right hand. But I was caught square around the back of my head by her fifth. I dropped to my knees, groggy. There was the sound of rushing air, then the round end of Arra's staff connected cleanly with the left side of my face and I went crashing to the ground.

The next thing I knew, I was staring up at the roof, surrounded by concerned vampires. "Darren?" Kurda asked, worry in his voice. "Are you all right?"

"What ... happened?" I wheezed.

"She knocked you out," he said. "You've been unconscious for five or six minutes. We were about to send for help."

I sat up, wincing at the pain. "Why's the room spinning?" I groaned.

Vanez laughed and helped me to my feet. "He'll be fine," the games master said. "A bit of concussion never killed a vampire. A good day's sleep and he'll be right as night."

"How much further is it to Vampire Mountain?" I asked weakly.

"The poor child doesn't know whether he's coming or going!" Kurda snapped, and started to lead me away.

"Wait!" I shouted, my head clearing a bit. I looked for Arra Sails and spotted her sitting on one of the bars, applying a cream to her bruised cheek. Shaking free of Kurda, I stumbled across to the vampiress and stood as firmly as I could before her.

"Yes?" she asked, eyeing me guardedly.

I stuck out a hand and said, "Shake."

Arra stared at the hand, then into my unfocused eyes. "One good fight doesn't make you a warrior," she said.

"Shake!" I repeated angrily.

"And if I don't?" she asked.

"I'll get back up on the bars and fight you till you do," I growled.

Arra studied me at length, then nodded and took my hand. "Power to you, Darren Shan," she said gruffly.

"Power," I repeated weakly, then fainted into her arms and knew no more till I came to in my hammock the next night.

CHAPTER EIGHTEEN

TWO NIGHTS after my encounter with Arra Sails, Mr Crepsley and me were called before the Vampire Princes. I was still stiff from my fight and Mr Crepsley had to help me dress. I groaned as I raised my arms over my head — ` they were black and blue from where I'd taken Arra's blows.

"I cannot believe you were foolish enough to challenge Arra Sails," Mr Crepsley tutted. He'd been teasing me about my fight with the vampiress since learning of it, although underneath his mocking front I could tell he was proud of me. "Even *I* would hesitate at going one on one with her on the bars."

"Guess that means I'm braver than you," I smirked.

"Stupidity and bravery are not the same thing," he chided me. "You could have been seriously injured."

"You sound like Kurda," I sulked.

"I do not agree with Kurda's views on the fighting ways of

vampires — he is a pacifist, which runs contrary to our nature — but he is correct when he says that sometimes it is better not to fight. When a situation is hopeless, and there is nothing at stake, only a fool battles on."

"But it wasn't hopeless!" I exclaimed. "I almost beat her!"

Mr Crepsley smiled. "You are impossible to talk to. But so are most vampires. It is a sign that you are learning. Now finish dressing and make yourself presentable. We must not keep the Princes waiting."

* * *

The Hall of Princes was situated at the highest internal point of Vampire Mountain. There was only one entrance to it, a long, wide tunnel guarded by a host of Mountain Guards. I hadn't been up here before — nobody could use the tunnel unless they had business in the Hall.

The green-garbed guards watched us every step of the way. You weren't allowed to take weapons into the Hall of Princes, or carry anything which might be used as a weapon. Shoes weren't permitted — too easy to hide a small dagger in the soles — and we were searched from head to foot at three different parts of the tunnel. The guards even ran combs through our hair, in case we had thin wires hidden inside!

"Why all the security?" I whispered to Mr Crepsley. "I thought the Princes were respected and obeyed by all vampires."

"They are," he said. "This is for tradition's sake more than anything else."

At the end of the tunnel we emerged into a huge cavern, in which a strange white dome stood gleaming. It was like no other building I'd ever seen — the walls pulsed, as though alive, and there were no joins or cracks that I could make out.

"What is it?" I asked.

"The Hall of Princes," Mr Crepsley said.

"What's it made of — rock, marble, iron?"

Mr Crepsley shrugged. "Nobody knows." He led me to the dome — the only guards on this side of the tunnel were grouped around the doors to the Hall — and told me to place my hands on it.

"It's warm!" I gasped. "And it throbs! What *is* it?"

"Long ago, the Hall of Princes was like any other," Mr Crepsley answered in his usual roundabout way. "Then, one night, Mr Tiny arrived and said he had gifts for us. This was shortly after the vampaneze had split from the vampires. The 'gifts' were the dome — which his Little People constructed, unseen by any vampire — and the Stone of Blood. The dome and Stone are magical artefacts. They—"

One of the guards at the doors hailed us. "Larten Crepsley! Darren Shan!" We hurried over. "You may be admitted now," the guard said, and struck the doors four times with the large spear he was carrying. The doors slid open — like electronic doors — and we entered.

Though no torches burned inside the Hall of Princes, it was as bright as day, far brighter than anywhere else in the mountain. The light originated in the walls of the dome itself, by means unknown to all but Mr Tiny. Long seats —

like pews – ran in circles around the dome. There was a large space at the centre, where four wooden thrones stood mounted on a platform. Three of the thrones were occupied by Vampire Princes. Mr Crepsley had told me that at least one Prince always skipped Council, in case anything happened to the others. Nothing hung from the walls, no paintings, portraits or flags. There were no statues either. This was a place for business, not pomp or ceremony.

Most of the seats were filled. Ordinary vampires sat at the rear; the middle sections were reserved for Mountain personnel, guards and the like. Vampire Generals occupied the front seats. Mr Crepsley and me made our way to the third row of seats from the front and slid in beside Kurda Smahlt, Gavner Purl and Harkat Mulds, who were waiting for us. I was glad to see the Little Person again, and asked what he'd been up to.

"Answering ... questions," he replied. "Saying same thing ... over and over ... and over ... again."

"Did any more of your memory come back?" I asked.

"No."

"But it's not for want of trying," Gavner laughed, leaning forward to squeeze my shoulder. "We've been practically torturing Harkat with questions, trying to get him to remember. And he hasn't complained once. If I was in his place, I'd have raised hell ages ago. He hasn't even been allowed to sleep!"

"Don't need ... much sleep," Harkat said shyly.

"Recovered from your bout with Arra yet?" Kurda asked.

Before I could answer, Gavner piped up. "I heard about that! What in Paradise were you thinking? I'd rather face a pit full of scorpions than hop on the bars with Arra Sails. I saw her make mincemeat of twenty seasoned vampires one night."

"It seemed like a good idea at the time," I grinned.

Gavner had to leave us to discuss something with a bunch of other Generals – vampires were forever debating serious issues in the Hall of Princes – and while we were waiting, Mr Crepsley explained a little more about the dome.

"The dome is magical. There is no way in except through the single set of doors. Nothing can penetrate its walls, no tool, explosive or acid. It is the toughest material known to man or vampire."

"Where did it come from?" I asked.

"We do not know. The Little People brought it in covered wagons. It took them months to haul it up, one sheet at a time. We were not allowed to watch as they assembled it. Our finest architects have been over it many times since, but not one can unravel its mysteries.

"The doors can only be opened by a Vampire Prince," he went on. "They can open them by laying their palms directly on the panels of the doors, or from their thrones, by pressing their palms down on the armrests."

"They must be electronic," I said. "The panels 'read' their fingerprints, right?"

Mr Crepsley shook his head. "The Hall was built centuries ago, long before electricity was even a thought in the minds of Man. It operates by paranormal means, or by a form of technology far advanced of anything we know.

"You see the red stone behind the Princes?" he asked. It was set on a pedestal five metres behind the platform, an oval stone, about twice the size of a football. "That is the Stone of Blood. That is the key, not only to the dome, but to the longevity of the vampire race itself."

"Long— what?" I asked.

"Longevity. It means long life."

"How can a stone have anything to do with a long life?" I asked, puzzled.

"The Stone serves several purposes," he said. "Every vampire, when accepted into the fold, must stand before the Stone and place his hands on it. The Stone looks as smooth as a ball of glass, but is ultra-sharp to the touch. It draws blood, which is absorbed by the Stone – hence its name – linking the vampire to the mental collective of the clan forever."

"Mental collective?" I repeated, wishing for the umpteenth time since I'd met Mr Crepsley that he'd use simple words.

"You know how vampires can mentally search for those they have bonded with?"

"Yes."

"Well, using the method of triangulation, we can also search for and find those we have *not* bonded with, via the Stone."

"Triangu— *what*?" I groaned, exasperated.

"Let us say you are a full-vampire whose blood has been absorbed by the Stone," he said. "When a vampire gives his blood, he also gives his name, by which the Stone and other vampires will thenceforth recognize him. If I want to search for you after you have been blooded, I merely place my hands on the Stone of Blood and think your name. Within seconds the Stone allows me to pinpoint your exact location anywhere on Earth."

"You could do this even if I didn't want to be found?" I asked.

"Yes. But pinpointing your location would be no good — by the time I got to where you had been when I made the search, you would have moved on. Hence the need for triangulation, which simply means three people are involved. If I wanted to find you, I could contact someone I was bonded with — Gavner, for instance — and mentally transmit your whereabouts to him. With me guiding him via the Stone of Blood, he could track you down."

I thought that over in silence a while. It was an ingenious system but I could see a few drawbacks. "Can anyone use the Stone of Blood to find a vampire?" I asked.

"Anyone with the ability to search mentally," Mr Crepsley said.

"Even a human or a vampaneze?"

"Very few humans have minds advanced enough to use the Stone," he said, "but the vampaneze have."

"Isn't the Stone dangerous then?" I asked. "If a vampaneze got his hands on it, couldn't he track every vampire down — at least all the ones he knew the names of — and guide his colleagues to them?"

Mr Crepsley smiled grimly. "Your battering at the hands of Arra Sails has not affected your powers of reasoning. You are correct — the Stone of Blood *would* mean the end of the vampire race if it fell into the wrong hands. The vampaneze would be able to hunt all of us down. They can also find those they do not know the names of — the Stone lets its user search for vampires by location as well as name, so they could scan for every vampire in England or America or wherever, then send out others to track them down. That is why we guard the Stone carefully and never let it leave the safety of the dome."

"Wouldn't it be simpler just to break it?" I asked.

Kurda, who'd been eavesdropping, laughed. "I put that proposal to the Princes several decades ago," he said. "The Stone could resist normal tools and explosives, the same as the walls of the dome, but that doesn't mean it's impossible to get rid of safely. 'Throw the damn thing down a volcano,' I pleaded, 'or toss it in the deepest sea.' They wouldn't hear of such a thing."

"Why not?" I asked.

"There are a number of reasons," Mr Crepsley answered before Kurda could reply. "First, the Stone can be used to locate vampires who are missing or in trouble, or those who are mad and on the loose. It is healthy to know that we are joined to the clan by more than tradition, that we can always rely on aid if we lead good lives, and punishment if we do not. The Stone keeps us in line.

"Second, the Stone of Blood is necessary to operate the

doors of the dome. When a vampire becomes a Prince, the Stone is a vital part of the ceremony. He forms a circle around it with two other Princes. They each use a hand to pump blood into him, while laying their other hand on the Stone. Blood flows from the old Princes to the new Prince, then to the Stone, and back again. By the end of the ceremony, the new Prince can control the doors of the Hall. Without the Stone, he would be a Prince in name only.

"There is a third reason why we do not destroy the Stone — the Lord of the Vampaneze." His face was dark. "The myth says that the Vampaneze Lord will wipe the vampire race from the face of the Earth when he comes to power, but through the Stone of Blood we might one night rise again."

"How's that possible?" I asked.

"We do not know," Mr Crepsley said. "But those were the words of Mr Tiny, and since the power of the Stone is also his, it makes sense to pay heed. Now more than ever, we must protect the Stone. Harkat's message concerning the Vampaneze Lord has struck at the hearts and spirits of many vampires. With the Stone, there is hope. To dispose of it now would be to surrender to fear."

"Charna's guts!" Kurda snorted. "I've no time for those old myths. We should get rid of the Stone, shut down the dome and build a new Hall of Princes. Apart from anything else, it's one of the main reasons the vampaneze are loathe to make a deal with us. They don't want to be hooked up to a magical tool of Mr Tiny's, and who can blame them? They're afraid of bonding with the Stone — they could never split from the vampire clan if they did, because we'd be able to use the Stone to hunt them down. If we removed the Stone, they might return to us, and then the vampaneze would be no more — there'd be one big family of vampires — and the threat of the Vampaneze Lord would evaporate."

"Does that mean you will be seeking to destroy the Stone when you are a Prince?" Mr Crepsley enquired.

"I'll mention the possibility," Kurda nodded. "It's a sensitive issue, and I don't expect the Generals to agree to it, but in time, as negotiations between ourselves and the vampaneze develop, I hope they'll come round to my way of thinking."

"Did you make this clear when you were seeking election?" Mr Crepsley asked.

Kurda shifted uncomfortably. "Well, no, but that's politics. Sometimes you have to hold things back. I didn't lie about it. If anyone had asked me for my views on the Stone, I'd have told them. They just ... didn't ... ask," he finished lamely.

"*Politics!*" Mr Crepsley huffed. "It is a sad day for vampires when our Princes voluntarily ensnare themselves in the despicable webs of politics." Sticking his nose in the air, he turned his back on Kurda and stared straight ahead at the platform.

"I've upset him," Kurda whispered to me.

"He's easily upset," I grinned. Then I asked if *I'd* have to bond with the Stone of Blood.

"Probably not until you become a full-vampire," Kurda said. "Half-vampires have been allowed to bond with it in the past, but not in the normal run of things."

I was going to ask more about the mysterious Stone of Blood and the dome, but then a serious-looking General banged the floor of the platform with a heavy staff and announced my name, along with Mr Crepsley's.

It was time to meet the Princes.

CHAPTER NINETEEN

THE THREE Vampire Princes in attendance were Paris Skyle, Mika Ver Leth, and Arrow. (The absent Prince was called Vancha March.)

Paris Skyle had a long grey beard, flowing white hair, no right ear, and he was the oldest living vampire at eight hundred earth years or more. He was revered by the others, not only for his immense age and position, but for his exploits when younger — according to the legends, Paris Skyle had been everywhere and done everything. Many of the tales were fanciful — he'd sailed with Columbus to America and introduced vampirism to the New World, fought beside Joan of Arc (a vampire sympathizer, apparently) and provided the inspiration for Bram Stoker's infamous *Dracula*. But that didn't mean the tales weren't true — vampires were, by their very existence, fanciful creatures.

Mika Ver Leth was the youngest Vampire Prince, a 'mere'

two hundred and seventy. He had shiny black hair and piercing eyes, like a raven's, and he dressed all in black. He looked even sterner than Mr Crepsley – his forehead was creased with wrinkles, as were the sides of his mouth – and I got the feeling he rarely smiled, if at all.

Arrow was a thickly-built bald man, with long tattoos of arrows adorning his arms and the sides of his head. He was a fearsome fighter, whose hatred of the vampaneze was legendary. He'd been married to a human before becoming a General, but she had been killed by a vampaneze who'd come to fight Arrow. He had returned to the fold, sullen and withdrawn, and trained to be a General. Since then he had devoted himself to his work, to the exclusion of all else.

All three Princes were burly, muscular men. Even the ancient Paris Skyle looked like he could toss an ox over his shoulder using a single hand.

"Greetings, Larten," Paris said to Mr Crepsley, stroking his long grey beard and studying the vampire with warm eyes. "It is good to see you in the Hall of Princes. I did not think I would look upon your face again."

"I vowed I would be back," Mr Crepsley replied, bowing before the Prince.

"I never doubted it," Paris smiled. "I just did not think I would be alive to welcome you. I have grown long of tooth, old friend. My nights are numbered."

"You will outlive us all, Paris," Mr Crepsley said.

"We shall see," Paris sighed. He fixed his gaze on me while Mr Crepsley bowed to the other Princes. When the vampire returned to my side, the old Prince said, "This must be your assistant — Darren Shan. Gavner Purl has spoken approvingly of him."

"He is of good blood and strong heart," Mr Crepsley said. "A fine assistant, who will one night make a first-rate vampire."

"'*One night*' indeed!" Mika Ver Leth snorted, squinting at me in a way I didn't like. "He's just a *boy*! This is no time for children to be admitted to our ranks. What possessed you to—"

"Please, Mika," Paris Skyle interrupted. "Let us not speak rashly. All here know the character of Larten Crepsley. We must treat him with the respect he has earned. I do not know why he chose to blood a child, but I am certain he can explain."

"I just think it's crazy, in this night and age." Mika Ver Leth grumbled his way to silence. When he was still, Paris turned to me and smiled.

"You must forgive us, Darren, if we seem discourteous. We are unused to children. It has been a long time since any were presented before us."

"I'm not really a child," I muttered. "I've been a half-vampire for eight years. It's not my fault my body hasn't aged."

"Precisely!" Mika Ver Leth snapped. "It's the fault of the vampire who blooded you. He—"

"Mika!" Paris snapped. "This vampire of noble standing and his assistant have come before us in good faith, to seek our approval. Whether we grant it or not, they deserve to be heard politely, not challenged rudely in front of their colleagues."

Mika collected himself, stood and bowed to us. "Sorry," he said through gritted teeth. "I spoke out of turn. I will not do so again."

A murmur spread through the Hall. From the whispers, I gathered that it was most unusual for a Prince to apologize to an inferior, especially one who was no longer a General.

"Come, Larten," Paris said, as chairs were brought forward for us. "Sit and tell us what you have been up to since last we met."

Once we were seated, Mr Crepsley ran through his story. He told the Princes of his association with the Cirque Du Freak, the places he'd been, the people he'd met. When he came to the part about Murlough, he asked to speak to the Princes in private. He told them in whispers of the mad vampaneze, and how we'd killed him. They were disturbed by the news.

"This is worrisome," Paris mused aloud. "If the vampaneze find out, they could use it as an excuse to start a war."

"How could they?" Mr Crepsley responded. "I am no longer part of the clan."

"If they were suitably enraged, they could overlook that," Mika Ver Leth said. "If the rumour of the Vampaneze Lord is true, we must tread very carefully where our blood cousins are concerned."

"Still," Arrow said, contributing to the conversation for the first time, "I don't think Larten erred. It would be different if he were a General, but as a free agent, he is not bound by our laws. Were I in his position, I'd have done the same thing. He acted discreetly. I don't think we can fault him for that."

"No," Mika agreed. Glancing at me, he added, "Not for *that*."

With the matter of Murlough out of the way, we returned to our chairs and raised our voices so that all in the Hall could hear.

"Now," Paris Skyle said, adopting a grave expression. "It is time we returned to the business of your assistant. We all know that the world has changed vastly these last few centuries. Humans are more protective of one another and their laws are stricter than ever, particularly with regard to their young. That is why we no longer blood children. Even in the past, we blooded few of them. It has been ninety years since we last added a child to our ranks. Tell us, Larten, why you decided to break with recent tradition."

Mr Crepsley cleared his throat and locked eyes with the Princes, one after the other, until they settled on Mika. "I have no valid reason," he said calmly, and the Hall erupted into barely-contained shouts and muffled, hurried conversations.

"There will be quiet in the Hall!" Paris shouted, and all noise ceased at once. He looked troubled when he faced us. "Come, Larten, do not play games. You would not blood a boy out of simple fancy. There must be a reason. Did you kill his parents, perhaps, and decide it was your place to take care of him?"

"His parents are alive," Mr Crepsley said.

"Both of them?" Mika snapped.

"Yes."

"Then they are looking for him?" Paris asked.

"No. We faked his death. They buried him. They think he is dead."

"That much at least you did right," Paris murmured. "But why blood him in the first place?" When Mr Crepsley didn't answer, he turned to me and asked, "Darren? Do *you* know why he blooded you?"

Hoping to bail the vampire out of trouble, I said, "I found out the truth about him, so maybe part of it was to protect himself — he might have figured that he had to make me his assistant or kill me."

"That is a reasonable excuse," Paris noted.

"But not the truth," Mr Crepsley sighed. "I was never afraid of being exposed by Darren. In fact, the only reason he discovered the truth about me was because I tried to blood a friend of his, a boy his own age."

The Hall erupted into controversy, and it took the barking Princes several minutes to quiet the vampires. When order was finally restored, Paris resumed the questioning, more troubled than ever. "You tried to blood *another* boy?"

Mr Crepsley nodded. "But his blood was tainted with evil — he would not have made a good vampire."

"Let me get this straight," Mika growled. "You tried blooding one boy, but couldn't; his friend found out, so you blooded him instead?"

"That is about the sum of it," Mr Crepsley agreed. "I also blooded him in a rush, without revealing the full truth of our ways, which was unpardonable. In my defence I will add that I studied him at great length before blooding him, and was convinced of his honesty and strength of character when I did."

"What drew you to the first boy — the one with evil blood?" Paris asked.

"He knew who I was. He had seen a portrait of me in an old book, drawn long ago when I was using the name of Vur Horston. He asked to become my assistant."

"Didn't you explain our ways to him?" Mika asked. "Didn't you tell him we don't blood children?"

"I tried, but..." Mr Crepsley shook his head miserably. "It was as though I had no control over myself. I knew it was wrong, but I would have blooded him regardless, if not for his foul blood. I cannot explain why, because I do not understand it."

"You'll have to come up with a better argument than that," Mika warned him.

"I cannot," Mr Crepsley said softly, "because I have none."

There was a polite cough behind us and Gavner Purl stepped forward. "May I intervene on my friend's behalf?" he asked.

"By all means," Paris said. "We welcome your input, if it can clear things up."

"I don't know if it can do that," Gavner said, "but I'd like to note that Darren is an extraordinary boy. He made the trek to Vampire Mountain – no small feat for one his age – and fought a bear poisoned with vampaneze blood along the way. I'm sure you have heard of his contest with Arra Sails a few nights ago."

"We have," Paris chuckled.

"He is bright and brave, wily and honest. I believe he has the makings of a fine vampire. Given the chance, I think he'll excel. He's young, but younger vampires than him have come through the ranks. You were only two years old when you were blooded, weren't you, Sire?" he asked Paris Skyle.

"That's not the point!" Mika Ver Leth shouted. "This boy could be the next Khledon Lurt and it wouldn't make a blind bit of difference. Facts are facts — vampires no longer blood children. It will set a dangerous precedent if we let this pass without taking action."

"Mika is right," Arrow spoke softly. "The boy's courage and ability are not the issue. Larten acted poorly in blooding the boy and we must address that."

Paris nodded slowly. "They speak the truth, Larten. It would be wrong of us to ignore this. You yourself would never have tolerated such a breach of the rules were you in our position."

"I know," Mr Crepsley sighed. "I do not seek forgiveness, merely consideration. And I ask that no reprisals be taken against Darren. The fault is mine, and I alone should be punished."

"I don't know about *punishment*," Mika said uncomfortably.

"I'm not out to make an example of you. Dragging your good name through the muck is the last thing on my mind."

"None of us wish to do that," Arrow agreed. "But what option have we? He did wrong — we must address that wrong."

"But we must address it mercifully," Paris mused.

"I ask for no mercy," Mr Crepsley said stiffly. "I am not a young vampire who acted out of ignorance. I expect no special treatment. If you decide I am to be executed, I will accept your verdict without complaint. If—"

"They can't kill you because of *me!*" I gasped.

"—If you decide I must be tested," he continued, ignoring my outburst, "I will rise to any challenge you care to set, and die meeting it if I must."

"There will be no challenge," Paris huffed. "We reserve challenges for those who have not proven themselves in battle. I will say once again — your good standing is not in question."

"Perhaps..." Arrow said hesitantly, then lapsed into silence. A few seconds later, he resumed. "I think I have it. The talk of challenges gave me an idea. There *is* a way to resolve this without killing our old friend or soiling his good name." Pointing a finger at me, he said coolly, "Let's set a challenge for the *boy.*"

CHAPTER TWENTY

THERE WAS a long, thoughtful silence. "Yes," Paris Skyle finally murmured. "A challenge for the boy."

"I said I did not want to bring Darren into this!" Mr Crepsley objected.

"No," Mika contradicted him. "You said you didn't want him to be *punished*. Well, he won't be — a challenge is not a punishment."

"It is fair, Larten," Paris agreed. "If the boy proves himself in a test, your decision to blood him will be accepted and no more need be said about it."

"And the dishonour will be *his* if he fails," Arrow added.

Mr Crepsley scratched his long facial scar. "It is an honest solution," he mused, "but the decision is Darren's, not mine. I will not force a challenge on him." He turned to me. "Are you prepared to prove yourself to the clan and clear our names?"

I fidgeted uneasily on my chair. "Um ... what sort of a

challenge are we talking about exactly?" I asked.

"A good question," Paris said. "It would be unfair to pit him in battle against one of our warriors — a half-vampire is no match for a General."

"And a quest would take too long," Arrow said.

"That leaves the Trials," Mika muttered.

"No!" someone shouted behind us. Looking around, I spotted a red-faced Kurda striding towards the platform. "I won't stand for this!" he stormed. "The boy isn't ready for the Trials. If you insist on testing him, let him wait till he is older."

"There will be no waiting," Mika growled, rising to his feet and taking a few steps towards Kurda. "*We* wield the authority here, Kurda Smahlt — you're not a Prince yet, so don't act like one."

Kurda stopped and glowered at Mika, then dropped to one knee and bowed his head. "My apologies for speaking out of turn, Sire."

"Apology accepted," Mika grunted, returning to his seat.

"Have I the permission of the Princes to speak?" Kurda asked.

Paris checked with Mika, who shrugged curtly. "You have," he said.

"The Trials of Initiation are for experienced vampires," Kurda said. "They were not designed for children. It wouldn't be fair to subject him to them."

"Life for vampires has never been *fair*," Mr Crepsley said. "But it can be *just*. I do not enjoy the idea of submitting

Darren to the Trials, but it is a just decision and I shall stand by it if he agrees."

"Excuse me," I said, "but what *are* the Trials?"

Paris smiled kindly at me. "The Trials of Initiation are tests for vampires who wish to become Generals," he explained.

"What would I have to do?"

"Perform five acts of physical courage," he said. "The tests are picked at random and are different for each vampire. One involves diving to the bottom of a deep pool and retrieving a dropped medallion. In another you must dodge falling boulders. In another you must cross a hall filled with burning coals. Some tests are more difficult than others, but none are easy. The risk is great, and though most vampires survive, death by misadventure is not unheard of."

"You mustn't agree to this, Darren," Kurda hissed. "The Trials are for full-vampires. You aren't strong, quick or experienced enough. You'll be signing your death warrant if you say yes."

"I disagree," Mr Crepsley said. "Darren *is* capable of passing the Trials. It will not be easy, and he may struggle, but I would not let him step forward if I thought he would be completely out of his depth."

"Let's vote on it," Mika said. "I say it's the Trials. Arrow?"

"I agree — the Trials."

"Paris?"

The oldest living vampire shook his head uncertainly. "Kurda has a point when he says the Trials are not for children. I trust your judgement, Larten, but fear your optimism is misplaced."

"Can you suggest another way?" Mika snapped.

"No, but..." Paris sighed deeply. "What do the Generals think?" he asked, addressing those in the Hall. "We have heard from Kurda and Mika. Does anyone else have anything to add?"

The Generals muttered among themselves, until a familiar figure stood and cleared her throat — Arra Sails. "I respect Darren Shan," she said. "I have shaken his hand, and those who know me know how much that means to me. I believe Gavner Purl and Larten Crepsley when they say he will be a valuable addition to our ranks.

"But I also agree with Mika Ver Leth — Darren must prove himself. All of us have had to endure the Trials. They help make us what we are. As a woman, the odds were stacked against me, but I overcame them and took my place in this Hall as an equal. There must be no exceptions. A vampire who cannot pull his own weight is of no use to us. We have no place for children who need to be wet-nursed and tucked into their coffins at daybreak.

"Having said that," she concluded, "I don't think Darren will let us down. I believe he will pass the Trials and prove himself. I have every confidence in him." She smiled at me, then glared at Kurda. "And those who say otherwise — those who'd wrap him in blankets — should not be heeded. To deny Darren the right of Trials would be to shame him."

"Noble words," Kurda sneered. "Will you repeat them at his funeral?"

"Better to die with pride than live in shame," Arra retorted.

Kurda cursed quietly to himself. "How about it, Darren?" he asked. "Will you face death just to prove yourself to these fools?"

"No," I said, and saw a pained look cross Mr Crepsley's face. "But I'll face death to prove myself to *me*," I added. When the red-cloaked vampire heard that, he beamed proudly and raised a clenched fist in salute.

"Let us put it to the Hall," Paris said. "How many think Darren should undertake the Trials of Initiation?" Every arm went up. Kurda turned aside in disgust. "Darren? You are willing to proceed?"

I looked up at Mr Crepsley and made a sign for him to bend down. In a whisper, I asked him what would happen if I said no. "You would be disgraced and sent from Vampire Mountain in shame," he said solemnly.

"Would you be shamed too?" I asked, knowing how much his good name meant to him.

He sighed. "In the eyes of the Princes I would not be, but in my own eyes I would. Having chosen and blooded you, I feel any shame of yours would also be mine."

I gave that careful consideration. I'd learnt a lot about Mr Crepsley, how he thought and lived, during the eight years I'd served as his assistant. "You couldn't bear such shame, could you?" I asked.

His expression softened. "No," he said quietly.

"You'd go and chase an early death. Hunt wild animals and fight vampaneze, and push yourself until one of them killed you?"

"Something along those lines," he agreed with a quick nod.

I couldn't let that happen. Six years ago, when we'd gone after Murlough, the mad vampaneze had kidnapped Evra, and Mr Crepsley had offered to trade his life for the snake-boy's. He'd have done the same for me if I'd fallen into the killer's hands. I didn't like the sound of these Trials, but if undertaking them meant Mr Crepsley could carry on without shame, I owed it to him to place myself in the firing line.

Facing the Princes, I stood up straight and said solidly, "I agree to the Trials."

"Then it is decided," Paris Skyle smiled approvingly. "Return tomorrow and we shall draw the first Trial. You may leave now and rest."

That was the end of our meeting. I left the Hall with Gavner, Harkat and Kurda. Mr Crepsley stayed to discuss business with the Princes — I think it had to do with Mr Tiny, Harkat's message and the dead vampaneze and vampire we'd found on our way here.

"I'm glad ... to leave at ... last," Harkat said as we made our way back to the Halls. "I was ... growing bored of ... same old ... scenery."

I smiled, then glanced at Gavner worriedly. "How tough

are these Trials?" I asked.

"Very," he sighed.

"Try tough as the walls of the Hall of Princes," Kurda growled.

"They're not *that* difficult," Gavner said. "Don't exaggerate the dangers, Kurda — you'll frighten him."

"That's the last thing I want to do," Kurda said, smiling encouragingly at me. "But the Trials are meant for fully-grown vampires. I spent six years preparing for them, like most vampires do, yet I only barely scraped through."

"Darren will be OK," Gavner insisted, though the doubt in his voice was only barely concealed.

"Besides," I laughed, trying to cheer Kurda up, "I can always drop out if I get in over my head."

Kurda stared hard at me. "Weren't you listening? Didn't you understand?"

"What do you mean?" I asked.

"Nobody walks away from the Trials," Gavner said. "You might fail, but you can't quit — the Generals won't let you."

"So I'll fail," I shrugged. "I'll throw in the towel if things get hairy — pretend I've twisted an ankle or something."

"He *doesn't* understand!" Gavner groaned. "We should have explained it fully before we let him agree. He's given his word now, so there's no going back. Black blood of Harnon Oan!"

"*What* don't I understand?" I asked, confused.

"In the Trials, failure entails one fate only — death!" Kurda told me grimly. I stared at him wordlessly. "Most who fail, die in the attempt. But should you fail and not die, you will be taken to the Hall of Death, strapped into a cage, hoisted above the pit, and—" he gulped, averted his eyes, and finished in a terrible whisper, "—*dropped on the stakes until you are dead!*"

TO BE CONTINUED…

THE SCORCHING SAGA
OF DARREN SHAN CONTINUES WITH...

TRIALS OF DEATH

There was a whistling sound close to my right. I jumped aside as fire blossomed in the air nearby, then ticked myself off — that burst had been close, but it wouldn't have struck. I should have stood my ground or edged carefully out of its way. Moving as I had, I could have stepped straight into trouble.

The flames were coming in quick bursts now, all around the Hall. I could feel a terrible heat building in the air and already it was hard to breathe. A hole a few centimetres from my right foot whistled. I didn't move as fire erupted and stung my leg — I could tolerate a small burn like that. A larger burst came out of a wider hole behind me. I shifted forward ever so slightly, rolling gently away from the worst of its bite. I felt the flames licking at the skin of my bare back, but none took hold.

The hardest times were when two or more geysers sprang from holes set close together. There was nothing I could do when trapped between a set of fiery pillars, except suck in my belly and step gingerly through the thinner wall of flames.

Within a few minutes my feet were in agony — they absorbed the worst of the flames. I spat on my palms and rubbed spit into my soles, which provided some measure of temporary relief. I would have stood on my hands to give my feet a rest, except that would have exposed my head of hair to the fire.

There was no way to keep track of time. I had to focus every last ounce of my concentration on the floor and fire. The briefest of distractions could have lethal consequences...

...I started back the way I'd come, but the fire was still shooting up through the holes, blocking my path. Reluctantly, I edged further towards the corner, ready to take the first opening as soon as one presented itself. The trouble was — none did.

The gurgling of pipes to my rear brought me to a halt. Flame burst out of the floor behind me, scorching my back. I grimaced but didn't move — there was nowhere to move to. The air was very poor in this region of the room. I waved my hands in front of my face, trying to create a draught which would suck some fresh air in, but it didn't work.

The pillars of flames in front of me had formed a virtual wall of fire now, at least two or three metres thick. I could barely see the rest of the room through the flickering flames. As I stood, waiting for a path to open, the mouths of the pipes at my feet hissed, several of them all at once. A huge ball of fire was on its way, about to explode directly underneath me! I had a split second to think and act.

Couldn't stand still — I'd burn.

Couldn't retreat — I'd burn.

Couldn't duck to the sides — I'd burn.

Forward, through the thick banks of fire? I'd probably burn, but there was open ground and air beyond — if I made it through. It was a lousy choice, but there was no time to complain. Closing my eyes and mouth, I covered my face with my arms and darted forward into the wall of crackling flames.

Fire engulfed and billowed about me like a ferocious red and yellow locust cloud. I'd never in my worst nightmare imagined such heat. I almost opened my mouth to scream. If I had, fire would have gushed down my throat and torched me to a crisp from the inside out.

DARREN SHAN

CIRQUE DU FREAK

THE SAGA OF DARREN SHAN
BOOK 1

Darren Shan is just an ordinary schoolboy – until he
gets an invitation to visit the Cirque Du Freak…
until he meets Madam Octa… until he comes face
to face with a creature of the night.

Soon, Darren and his friend Steve are caught in a
deadly trap. Darren must make a bargain with the
one person who can save Steve. But that person is
not human and only deals in blood…

ISBN 978 0 00 675416 9

www.darrenshan.com

DARREN SHAN

THE VAMPIRE'S ASSISTANT

THE SAGA OF DARREN SHAN
BOOK 2

Darren Shan was just an ordinary schoolboy – until his visit to the Cirque Du Freak. Now, as he struggles with his new life as a Vampire's Assistant, he tries desperately to resist the one thing that can keep him alive… blood. But a gruesome encounter with the Wolf Man may change all that…

ISBN 978 0 00 675513 5

www.darrenshan.com

DARREN SHAN

TUNNELS OF BLOOD

**THE SAGA OF DARREN SHAN
BOOK 3**

Darren Shan, the Vampire's Assistant, get's a taste of city life when he leaves the Cirque Du Freak with Evra and Mr Crepsley. At night the vampire goes about secret business, while by day Darren enjoys his freedom.

But then bodies are discovered... Corpses drained of blood... The hunt for the killer is on and Darren's loyalties are tested to the limit as he fears the worst. One mistake and they are all doomed to perish in the tunnels of blood...

ISBN 978 0 00 675514 2

www.darrenshan.com

DARREN SHAN

TRIALS OF DEATH

THE SAGA OF DARREN SHAN
BOOK 5

The Trials: seventeen ways to die unless the luck of the vampires is with you. Darren Shan must pass five fearsome Trials to prove himself to the vampire clan – or face the stakes in the Hall of Death.

But Vampire Mountain holds hidden threats. Sinister, potent forces are gathering in the darkness. In this nightmare world of bloodshed and betrayal, death may be a blessing...

ISBN 978 0 00 711440 5

www.darrenshan.com